Rosalee

SARAH LAMB

A thank you to my proofreader, Brooke, and all of the lovely women who help ARC read to catch those typos I miss!

This book was not written by AI. Any typos are proudly (and embarrassingly!) my own human created ones!

This book is not allowed to be used in training AI.

Paperback ISBN: 978-1-960418-45-6

Large print ISBN: 978-1-960418-46-3

Contents

Life is full of twists, turns, and sometimes unfairness. But I hope as your story unfolds, you find happiness, contentment, and the perfect ever after.

Chapter 1

About twenty miles outside of Spring Falls, Kansas, 1880

The sound of laughter from her mother's dinner guests tickled Rosalee Milton's ears as voices drifted through the open window. Outside on their back porch she stood, hidden in the shadows. The sweet fragrance from the large flower garden carried toward her on the breeze. Peonies, roses, night blooming jasmine.

Rosalee wrapped her arms around herself and breathed in the cool evening air, enjoying the moment of solitude. There weren't enough of those quiet minutes in her day.

Briefly, she closed her eyes, blocking out the sight of her father's large estate. It was foolish, but she entertained a child's hope that when she reopened them, it would all just be a dream. That peace would surround her, and the chaos behind her wouldn't exist. There was too much of it suffocating her. Even her new silk dinner gown felt like it was confining her, pulling at her neck, at her chest, at her soul.

Rosalee didn't know what to do, or even what was going on. As of late, she felt like she was struggling to entertain the frequent guests her mother had, which was odd, seeing as it was something she'd enjoyed her entire life. For some reason Rosalee couldn't fathom, she'd found it more difficult to smile and make small talk and flatter people she had no interest in knowing.

If only Andrew Radcliffe had accepted her suggestion of marriage. After all, they each had their own interests, and a marriage of convenience would have been wonderfully convenient for both of them. She could have traveled, which was the thing she enjoyed most, and he could have done whatever it was he did on his ranch.

Besides, they were friends. That counted for something, didn't it? In fact, at one time she had thought they'd marry. But life had separated them, they quite honestly weren't suited, and by the time she thought of her idea, he was in love with someone else.

Oh, she couldn't fault him. And Evie was a lovely woman, and perfect for Andrew. But as Rosalee had hugged her friends tightly at their wedding, a hollow had filled her. And it had just grown worse over the last few months. Now, it was a gnawing ache almost constantly. She just couldn't place her finger on what, exactly, it was.

It wasn't for marriage. No, if Rosalee had wanted to be married, she could have been, easily. In fact, she'd avoided the whole idea as much as she could, but her parents had been pressing her for the last few weeks. Making comments that if she didn't choose someone, they'd choose for her. It was preposterous. But also a possibility.

No, the ache was likely because Andrew was happy. He deserved it, he did. But he'd found love. And it seemed unlikely that was something she'd ever get. She was a woman, bound to accept whatever was given to her. Love wasn't something she could ever hope for. Even marital kindness might be too much to expect.

Rosalee pressed her lips together. Her father had been hinting strongly as of late about her need to leave home, and if he came right out and told her that she would be getting married, Rosalee wasn't sure how she could avoid her fate. She was a woman with little say in her own life. She supposed she'd been lucky until now. With her father's work travels taking him away so much, and very few men around her age who could offer much in exchange for her hand, she'd been able to stay, happily, unwed.

If only it could stay that way for a long, long time. Then, perhaps, there would be the smallest of chances she could find what Andrew had. Happiness. Love.

She took another deep breath. It was time to go back inside. But before she could turn, a figure in the distance caught her eye. It was a stable hand her father had brought on. He was leading one of the horses back to a pasture. She'd never talked to him before, but she had noticed him many times. She also envied him. The freedom to choose one's own life? Choose what you wanted to do? Even if that was simply to work for someone else. That was her dream.

Rosalee slipped back inside the house, where she spent the next hour laughing at the same stories she'd heard a dozen times, listening to the piano player her mother had hired playing the same music they always played, and hoping the throbbing in her temples would abate.

It wasn't until she was tucked in her bed that Rosalee felt as though she could relax. The day had been long, and tomorrow was likely to be the same. It was good to be alone and have a chance to rest. She yawned, and was just about to drift off, when she heard shouting outside her door, and the thundering of footsteps in the hallway.

Alarmed, she grabbed her dressing gown, hastily throwing it over her nightdress, and opened her door. A few paces away, she saw her mother, still fully dressed, rushing toward the stairs. "Mother?" Rosalee asked.

"An outbuilding is on fire," her mother said, as she hurried down the stairs. "I don't know if the house is in danger. Your father is outside."

Rosalee followed her mother, and as they raced through a side door and to the place Rosalee had been just hours before, the smell of smoke hit her face. It stung her eyes and burned her lungs. Tiny sparks flew through the night sky, like the small bugs that would light the sky on a summer's night.

Flames had overtaken one half of a small building used for storage, and men were lined up, throwing buckets of water at it with all the speed they could muster.

Her father stood, watching grimly. "What happened?" Rosalee asked as she approached him.

He just shook his head, and gestured for another bucket to be passed along the line. "Don't know. There's no time to ask."

The heat of the flames reached her, even at the distance of a hundred feet, and every male there on the ranch passed buckets of water or smacked at smoldering spots on the ground with wet sacks in a desperate attempt to keep the fire from spreading.

By some miracle, the fire was extinguished an hour later. A watch was set, to be sure the devastated building wouldn't reignite. Unsettled by the event, Rosalee went in search of some tea from Cook before going back to bed. She wondered how the fire had started. She'd wanted to move closer to the damage herself, to see if something caught her eye, but her mother had told her to get back in the house, as it was unseemly for her to be outside in her dressing gown.

Rosalee had complied, though she'd rolled her eyes. It seemed that something as important as a fire could be an excuse for one not to be dressed in their finery, but it appeared that wasn't the case. She admitted to herself, it likely wasn't appropriate to be seen in so little, but the men in her father's employ had quickly vacated once the flames were out. Who was there to notice?

Tea in hand, she tiredly moved toward the stairs to go to her bedroom. She assumed her mother was settling in to sleep. Father would be up, of course, perhaps talking to the men who worked for him. However, upon hearing familiar voices from her father's study, Rosalee paused. She could hear her parents' muffled words through the thick oak door. Her father sounded agitated, though she couldn't make out the whole of what he was saying.

Rosalee didn't blame him. What had happened was terrible. In the morning, the full extent of the damage would be seen, and she hoped that there had not been any lives lost or injuries among the men or animals. Items could be replaced. Lives could not.

Just then, her mother's loud gasp froze Rosalee in her tracks. Her mother was never excitable. For some reason, the sound made Rosalee's heart race. The delicate teacup fell from Rosalee's hands, shattering on the hardwood floor. The study door opened a second later, and her parents stood, looking at her as she kneeled, trying to pick up the shards among the puddles of tea.

"I'm sorry," Rosalee said. "I'm still trembling from the fire. My tea slipped as I was going back to my room."

She wasn't sure that they believed her, but her father gruffly said, "That's all right. While you are here, there's something I want to tell you."

"What is that?" Rosalee asked, nodding her thanks to a maid who swiftly arrived and cleared away the mess.

"You will be traveling tomorrow, to your aunt Cynthia's home back East. Your mother and I will join you, once she's helped me take care of a business matter. We'll be a few days behind you." Her father checked his pocket watch. "You will take the noon stage to the train station. I'll have one of the hands take you to town tomorrow morning."

"Tomorrow? But that's not enough time to pack," Rosalee said. "What should I bring? Will we be attending any events? Why so suddenly? What of the party we are to host next week?"

"It will be postponed," her mother said. Her eyes darted to Rosalee's father. "This is much more important. As for the rest..."

Rosalee wanted to ask more questions. Like, what kind of business matter was her mother helping with? She had never had any dealings in Father's businesses before, but the look on her father's face and the slight shake of her mother's head stopped her from saying more.

"Just pack what you need," her mother said, her voice sounding falsely cheerful. "We'll take advantage of being there in Boston to update our wardrobes. My sister Cynthia knows a wonderful dressmaker."

Rosalee nodded uneasily, keeping her concerns inside as she bid her parents goodnight. Something about the situation didn't feel right. Was her father's insistence that they leave because of the fire? Did he fear for their safety? He was a man who sometimes made enemies. That was natural in business, he had said. Perhaps this had been a warning?

Back in her room, Rosalee stood at her window. There was a full moon, and it illuminated the men walking around the grounds, keeping watch for signs of the fire returning. A shiver ran through her at the realization she didn't know any of the men her father employed. Did he know them all? More importantly, did he trust them?

If this was arson, it could have been done by any one of them. Was the house next? Suddenly, her reluctance to leave and the questions brought up by her parents' strange behavior fled. Rosalee couldn't wait to travel to safety.

Chapter 2

As he poured water over still-steaming coals, Aaron Woods watched as the Milton family returned to their house. It was impossible not to glare at the retreating figures, especially that of Mr. Milton. How many lives had Albus Milton ruined to get where he was, Aaron wondered. Certainly his.

The fire tonight had been unexpected. Had it not been such a serious thing for the men putting it out, he might have laughed at the man's dose of misfortune. He was owed it. In truth, Aaron didn't care if the Miltons were inconvenienced. They wouldn't miss the money it would take to replace whatever was damaged.

They deserved it. Uptight, dripping in more money than could take a lifetime to spend, and stepping on the shoulders of whoever it took to get where they wanted to go. What he didn't understand was why so many people liked them. Spoke highly of them. He didn't. But he knew the real Albus Milton. So did others who worked for him or were in business with him. Only, no one dared to do anything about it. Not even the men who were underpaid or threatened.

Heck, Aaron was no better than them. Forced here, and taking it. Not standing up for himself.

He let his scowl rest on each of the Miltons in turn. Mrs. Milton. A tall, thin woman with a pinched face. He didn't know much beyond the fact she was the typical society woman. Looked down her nose at everyone. Even her own daughter.

Their daughter, Rosalee, she was pretty. Dark hair, a sweet face. The kind of woman everyone stared at. Even Aaron couldn't help but find his eyes drawn to her each time she was near. He'd never spoken to her, though. Rosalee was old enough to be married, but still lived at home. He figured it was because no one wanted her. She was likely the perfect mix of her parents. All the bad parts, and, as far as he was concerned, they had nothing good in them. Especially her father.

Mr. Milton was a man who got what he wanted every time. A man who had his fingers in lumber, ore, cattle, horses...there was more, too, Aaron was willing to bet. Maybe not all of it was legal, either. He owned several successful and large businesses in the West, and several in the East. He was always traveling to one or the next, while his wife and daughter kept busy entertaining themselves and others with lavish parties.

Aaron couldn't stand the family, but most of all the patriarch. Who—who was turning back toward where Aaron was raking the coals, trying to see they cooled and didn't flare up again. Quickly, he looked away, trying to cool his temper.

"Aaron," Mr. Milton called, coming up alongside of him. "A word."

It took every bit of him not to grit his teeth as he answered. "Sir."

"I have a job for you," the man said.

"You already gave me one," Aaron answered, leaning on the rake. Anger seethed through him, hot like the fire had been. "One I didn't ask for. Didn't want. That's why I'm here at your place, instead of my own. Looking after your land, not mine. Your animals. Not the ones I bred."

His boss was quiet, and looked around. There were a few men nearby, but not close enough to overhear them. Not that it mattered. They likely had their own stories of why they were there. He was just another one.

"This is different."

Aaron finally looked into Mr. Milton's face. The smug expression he wore each time he looked at Aaron wasn't there. Perhaps the fire had humbled him. Maybe he knew it could have been his house, especially if it had been a windy night. The man was lucky. Too lucky. And he got that by taking it from others.

"What's in it for me?" Aaron asked. He shrugged a shoulder, wiping away the smoke from his forehead. This shirt was going to be ruined. Another thing destroyed because of a Milton.

Mr. Milton crossed his arms. His voice was cold as he answered. "You owe me, boy."

"I think we both know that's not true," Aaron answered, meeting the man's eyes. "You know as well as I do what happened that night."

"Doesn't matter. That's what the law says," his boss replied. "At my word, you could be in jail." But before Aaron could answer, Mr. Milton held up a hand. "Or, you do this, and I'll clear your debt."

That got his attention. Aaron gave him a considering look. "It's an unfair debt," he said.

"And it could be cleared. Completely. We'd never have to see each other again."

That sure was tempting. But Aaron was quiet a moment, thinking before he answered. A man didn't just forgive something like that. Not without wanting something steep in return. He'd never known Mr. Milton to be a fair man. Or honest. He took his time before he answered, "What's the job? It's not a yes; I just want to know. Might be better than being here the next four years."

Mr. Milton nodded stiffly. "My daughter will be heading East in the morning. You are to make sure she gets there. No matter what. Safe and sound, or kicking and screaming. It doesn't matter to me which. There's a good deal depending on her arrival."

"You want me to babysit her?" Aaron knew his voice was incredulous.

"No. I don't want her to know you are following her. You won't even talk to her, if she does what she's supposed to. Your job is to see she gets there, at any cost. I hope it won't come to you forcing her, but if it does, you have my permission to do what you need to."

Aaron felt his eyebrows twitch. "You think she won't go?"

For the first time he'd ever seen it, Aaron watched as Mr. Milton's expression turned to one of hesitation. Concern. Worry. And he liked seeing that. It made him feel good, knowing he might be able to have some small shred of power over the man who'd ruined his life.

"Rosalee is..." The man was quiet for a moment. "My daughter can be headstrong. As long as she doesn't find out why we are sending her to her aunt, all will be well. But there are dangers for a woman traveling alone. That's why I want you there."

"Begging your pardon," Aaron said, filled with curiosity. "Why don't you just take her yourself?"

"We'll be traveling a few days behind her, my wife and I," Mr. Milton said, not meeting his eyes. "But there's something we need to attend to first."

"The reason she's being sent East," Aaron guessed with a smirk. "She doesn't know what that is, and you bet the moment she does or suspects, she won't go."

"Will you see she gets there or not?" Mr. Milton asked.

Aaron nodded, and set the rake against the charred side wall. "Sure will. Expenses paid and then some. In advance. But I want it in writing that my debt to you is clear, and once she's there, I don't ever want to set eyes on you again." He stepped closer. "I'll never forgive you for what you did to me."

Mr. Milton nodded. "You'll have it. Wait for me in Boston. I'll just be a few days behind. Once I see my daughter, in writing, you'll have my word." He hesitated. "For what it's worth, I didn't mean for things to turn out this way. It was a heat-of-the-moment mistake."

"You could have put a stop to it," Aaron said, his voice tight, and his hands curled into fists at his sides. "But you didn't. And that's what I won't forgive."

The older man nodded once. "I understand." He hesitated again, and then warned, "I'm trusting you to take care of my daughter."

Aaron didn't answer. He just watched silently as Mr. Milton turned toward his large house, then turned to go pack his bag. Someone else could watch over the smoldering pile before him. He didn't know why the man was asking him to watch over his daughter. But he knew the reason he'd said yes. He'd lost almost a year of his life to the Milton family. Another week wouldn't hurt. Then, he'd be free.

Les, the foreman, and someone Aaron would consider a friend, stepped from the shadows. "Heard the whole thing," he said with a slow headshake. "That girl sure isn't gonna be happy."

"I'm not sure anyone ever is, with his decisions," Aaron said, jerking his head toward their boss.

"I'll miss you," Les said. "You're the hardest working man here. Most honest, too."

"I've learned a lot from you," Aaron said, offering his hand and shaking the foreman's. "I appreciate it."

"While I don't know how you've been wronged," Les said, "as it's your business and not mine, I just want to tell you that you're a good man. I know it sure as the sun will rise, and I'm right sorry."

The foreman walked away before Aaron could answer. He swallowed back the lump of emotion. The foreman was a good man, too, and his words meant a lot.

Aaron stirred at the ash again before setting down the rake, and returned his thoughts toward tomorrow. He'd be gone. Get his freedom.

Rosalee Milton might be an entitled, snooty woman, but she was also, by all appearances, obedient. How much trouble could it be to see she got back East safely?

Chapter 3

Rosalee had spent the last hour hurriedly packing as much as she could into her travel trunks. She disliked not knowing what to take, how long she'd be gone, and what she might need to wear. This was most unlike her parents, her mother especially. Usually, every detail was planned down to the smallest thing with a good deal of notice.

But, if last night's fire had anything to do with the reason why there was such a rush to leave, she wasn't going to argue. She was simply going to pack her favorite dresses and hope nothing happened to the rest. She bit her lip as she wondered if she should remove the blue day dress to try and squeeze in the green silk.

A knock sounded, and her mother walked in without waiting for Rosalee's invitation. All thoughts of dresses left Rosalee's mind. "Are you packed?" her mother asked, pausing at the large mirror and smoothing her hair.

"Just about. It would have been helpful if I had been given more notice," Rosalee said, closing her jewelry box and taking it to a trunk. "I don't feel prepared. I've tried to pack for every occasion, but I still feel as though I've forgotten things. Or that I don't have enough room. Are you sure I can't have just one more trunk?"

"I know, dear, but there just wasn't enough notice to properly plan out everything. Your father didn't get the marriage offer until yesterday," her mother said, peering closely at herself in the mirror. "And he doesn't want Mr. Webster to back out of the deal. Men simply don't understand all that goes into something like this. We will just buy whatever else you need."

The scarf Rosalee had been folding slipped from her grasp. Every inch of her felt chilled. Slowly, she turned. "What did you say?" she whispered. "Marriage? I...I thought you wanted us to leave because of the fire. In case it wasn't an accident."

Her mother tittered, "Whatever would make you think such a thing? Of course it was an accident. Done by a careless employee who has now been let go." Then, she brought her hands to her mouth. "Oh no," she said worriedly. "I wasn't supposed to say anything about your upcoming nuptials. Your father wanted it to be a surprise." She smiled at Rosalee. "Surprise! I know you are likely excited. However, please act as though you don't know anything. You know how he gets."

"It's too late for that," Rosalee said grimly. "And you know that I am not the least bit excited. Tell me everything. I deserve to know."

Her mother looked distressed, but then smiled. It wasn't a real smile. It was that one she wore when she had terrible news, but was trying to pretend like all was well. "You've had a marriage offer," she said brightly. "And your father said yes."

"What did you say about backing out of a deal?" Rosalee demanded. "What deal?"

Her mother twisted her fingers together nervously. When she realized what she was doing, she smoothed her dress instead, and strode over to inspect one of the open trunks. "Your father has wanted this merger for a long time," she said, not answering Rosalee's question, as she ran a hand over one of the packed dresses. "It's a wonderful opportunity."

"And I'm what gets the signature on the dotted line?"

"In a manner of speaking." Her mother shrugged. Then, her face lit up. "But he's quite old. Perhaps you won't be married long before you're a rich widow. Won't that be nice? Then you can get what you want. To be single and travel. But you'll be more respectable by then and, as a widow, be allowed to do more."

Rosalee's eyes narrowed. "Just how old is old?"

"Does it matter?" her mother asked, walking over and snapping one of the trunks shut. "We'll get your wedding trousseau while back East."

"Mother," Rosalee said, hating the tone that crept into her voice. It almost reeked of pleading. "Please. Won't you tell me?"

Her mother was quiet and refused to meet Rosalee's eyes. Finally, she said, "I was told he's a...a few years older than your father. Perhaps ten. Or so. But not more than twenty."

Rosalee all but collapsed on her bed. It was bad enough they'd arranged a marriage without any input from her. It was worse that it was part of a business deal. But to choose a man older than her father? Someone potentially old enough to even be her grandfather?

It happened, she knew it did. Sometimes, such a marriage even went well. But usually, it didn't. No older man took issue with a much younger wife. Then again, it wasn't the man who would suffer. Perhaps some women did it, hoping to bide their time until they became a rich widow, but there were no guarantees. Besides, that just sounded cruel and cold. If it wasn't to be a marriage of convenience, that Rosalee entered into freely, she wanted one of love.

"Why would you do this to me?" she asked, sure she was in shock because right now, all she felt was disbelief. A strange numbness was filling her.

"Because," her mother hissed fiercely, her eyes blazing, "your father needs that business deal. He's lost a great deal of money recently, and this merger will remedy that." She fixed Rosalee with a stern look. "You've had the last twenty-six years to do whatever you wanted. Now, it's time you do what you should, and help your family."

"At the cost of my happiness?" Rosalee argued. "So, I get no say whatsoever? You really think it's acceptable to have me marry a man older than Father? You'd do that to me?"

"If you'd wanted a say," her mother said, her voice sharp, "you'd have chosen a husband sooner. You did not, and so we have chosen one for you. That is the way of things. You are beyond lucky your father has been so agreeable for so long. Most young women would not be so fortunate. You are a spinster, Rosalee. To the rest of the world, that means you are either undesirable or of ill reputation. How does that make our family look?"

"I won't do it," Rosalee said around the lump in her throat. Her voice wobbled, and she hated herself for it. Better to be thought as unwanted or even a loose woman.

"You'll do what you must," her mother said. Her tone softened slightly, and she reached a hand out to Rosalee, though she didn't touch her. "Women must make sacrifices. That is the way of things. But, it might not turn out as badly as you think. Take heart, dear. Give it a chance. You've really no choice but to try and make the best of it. It's what women must do."

Footsteps sounded in the hallway, and her mother held her finger to her lips and shook her head slightly. Rosalee nodded. She understood. That was her mother's way of saying not to speak more. Truthfully, Rosalee was more than happy to pretend she didn't know her parents were about to force her into marriage. This was one secret she'd gladly keep. Perhaps she could buy herself some time to get them to change their minds.

Before she had time to think further, her father appeared, with two of the men in his employ behind him. "Time to go. What's taking so long?"

Rosalee looked on quietly as her trunks were taken from her room. She glanced around as she followed her parents out of the room. Would she ever see it again? If they had their way, she'd likely only come back as a married woman. Her parents wouldn't prevent her from getting her belongings, but last night might have been the final one in her bed. Alone in her room.

"Rosalee was asking about the fire," her mother said, resting her hand on her husband's arm. She let out a small laugh. The one she gave when she was nervous and trying to hide it. "She was concerned that's why we were leaving. I was trying to ease her mind."

"Nothing more than a careless mistake," her father answered, looking at Rosalee over his shoulder. "The man responsible will pay for all the damages."

"As he should," her mother sniffed. "Imagine treating another's property so callously!"

Her father grunted, but didn't say more. It was on the tip of Rosalee's tongue to say she felt like someone's property, but she wasn't supposed to know what was about to happen to her. She was sure that's why her mother had brought up the fire.

Rosalee watched as her trunks were loaded. Her father helped her into the carriage. "Here is your stage ticket, and your train ticket is being held for you at the station." He nodded to the driver, a young boy of perhaps fifteen who she'd seen around the stable a few times. "Pete will drive you."

She nodded, not wanting to meet her father's eyes, for fear he'd know that she knew something.

"We'll be right behind you," her mother said, leaning forward to embrace her. Before Rosalee could move back, her mother squeezed her arms painfully. In a low voice, she said, "You will get on that train. Do you understand?"

"Yes, Mother," Rosalee said.

Her mother nodded, looking satisfied, and released her. Rosalee sat stiffly, head pointing forward as they started the drive toward town. She didn't have long to think of a plan. There was no way she was getting on that train to go East, and she wasn't marrying Mr. Webster.

Chapter 4

Aaron watched from a distance as the carriage drove toward town, Miss Milton inside and Pete at the reins. His saddlebag was packed, and he rode the mare Mr. Milton had loaned him. As if it weren't a parting jab, it was the mare that should have been his. The one he'd been inspecting—not stealing—when the man had accused him and turned his life upside down.

Something stronger than resentment boiled inside him, and a bitter taste filled his mouth. Didn't matter. In a few days, that would all be behind him. He'd see Milton's daughter made it East, then wash his hands of the family, start over, and build his business from the ground up. And this time, he'd succeed.

Aaron let his eyes roam over the distant figures. He wondered why Miss Milton was sitting so stiffly. This morning, as she'd climbed in, her lips had been pressed together and her eyes were flashing, as though she were upset about something. He wondered why. What could a woman like that have to be upset about, ever?

Well, maybe the getting married off, if she wasn't wanting it. But as far as he knew, she didn't know about that part, so he was sure that wasn't it.

The town rose ahead, and Aaron rode past the carriage, dropping the mare at the livery. As he pulled his saddlebags free, he sighed and ran a hand along her neck. "Not your fault, girl, but you'd have been the start of my stock. Wish you had been. At the same time, wish we'd never have met."

A lump in his throat, he turned toward the stage. Miss Milton stood there, a look on her face he couldn't decipher, and Pete watched that her trunks were loaded. Once they were, she climbed in the stage, and a moment later, Aaron got on after her, unfolding a newspaper. He held it in front of his face, hoping that if the woman looked over, she wouldn't see him.

It was a full coach, with eight squeezed inside, and two more atop. The driver shut the door, and as he swung up to his seat, the stage rocked slightly. There was the crack of a whip, and they rumbled toward the next stop, about an hour and a half away.

Aaron must have dozed. When he woke, he saw Miss Milton staring at him. She flushed, then looked away.

Tiredly, he wiped a hand over his mouth, making sure he hadn't been doing something embarrassing like drooling. He'd been dreaming about his ma's blackberry pie. He missed her. Hadn't been home since the accusation. He didn't want her to know and bring shame to her.

Aaron yawned and longed to stretch out his stiff limbs. Next to him, a rotund man snored, and on his other side, a woman knitted. The click, click, click of her needles created a certain tone that made his ears feel funny.

The stage slowed, and everyone tried to peer through the windows at once. Aaron caught sight of the small town of Cottonwood Falls. He didn't know too much about the place, but it looked nice enough.

"We'll stop for thirty minutes," the driver said as he opened the door. With a jerk of his head, he added, "Facilities are over there."

One by one, the passengers climbed out. Aaron tried to keep his eye on Miss Milton, but when she headed toward the area that was obviously the station's ladies privy, he averted his eyes.

A bakery a few doors away called to him, and he hurried over to get a bite to take with him, not knowing when they'd stop next. He was hungry. Hastily, he ordered and then left with two small hand pies, one apple, one onion, and headed back to the stagecoach where the other passengers were climbing back in.

He joined them, but as he settled into his seat, Aaron noticed Rosalee Milton wasn't anywhere to be seen. The driver started to shut the door.

"Wait a second," Aaron said, pushing it back open as he climbed out. "You're missing someone."

"I ain't," the driver corrected. "Ain't no one else getting on."

"There was a woman, one in a lavender dress," Aaron said, glancing about.

The driver shrugged. "Had her trunks taken down. Now, I've got to go. Are you coming or ain't you?"

"I'm staying," Aaron said, jumping up to the stage roof to get his saddlebag. "I was tasked with seeing she got where she needed to go."

The driver shrugged. "None of my concern. But I'm leaving. You'd best get down." He swung into the seat, and Aaron jumped off the stage just as it flew away.

His bag in hand, Aaron stood in the middle of the small town. As he glanced around, the sign over the station caught his eyes. *Cottonwood Falls*, it proclaimed, *the place where dreams come true.*

"Not mine," Aaron muttered. "This is a nightmare. Where did that woman go?"

"Lose someone?" a man asked, pausing as he started to walk past.

"I might have," Aaron said. "A woman in a lavender dress with dark hair. She had two trunks, so she couldn't have gone far."

To his relief, the man nodded. "I saw her. She went past my practice a few moments ago. Someone was carrying her trunks to the boarding house across the street. Welcome to town."

"Your practice? The boarding house?" Aaron realized he was repeating the man, but he felt confused as he looked out over the unfamiliar town, his eyes searching for a sign to direct him. "Where might that be?"

The man pointed. "Right there. That's the boarding house. I'm Dr. Edward Mason. My home and office are just across the street." He gestured to a large white house.

"Ah, thank you," Aaron said. He offered his hand. "Aaron Woods. I appreciate it."

The doctor nodded curiously. "I hope you catch up to your wife," he said.

"She's—" Aaron was about to say she wasn't his wife, but how would that sound? A stranger off the stage following a woman? He might get arrested, and then he'd never get her back East so he could continue on his way. There was a lot of lost time to make up for.

"She's impatient," he said instead, with a laugh. "Anxious to wash off the travel dust."

"I understand that. Well, if either of you need anything, stop by. My wife, Caroline, is also a doctor," Edward

Mason said, and then nodded a farewell as he strode toward a building.

Aaron watched him for a moment. A woman doctor? It sounded like a good idea to him, and it was pretty special that this place had two doctors. They were lucky.

He headed toward the boarding house. It was a yellow building, with a white door, flowers in pots on the front porch, and some worn-looking rocking chairs that were empty.

A sign read: *Rooms for rent.* Just before he raised his hand to knock, he noticed the curtain pulled back enough that he could see inside. Rosalee Milton had handed a woman some money, and in turn was being handed a key.

Aaron groaned. It looked like she had no intention of getting on that train. He knew her father said he could drag her there kicking and screaming, but that wasn't really an option. The man had just said that, right? Aaron closed his eyes. He had been so close to his freedom. Now what was he going to do?

Chapter 5

As Rosalee walked up the stairs of the boarding house, she tried not to let the constant chatter of the owner grate on her nerves. She was feeling anxious over her situation, and wanted quiet. It appeared that wasn't going to be an option here.

"And if you need anything else, just let me know," Mrs. Harper finished.

"Thank you, I will," Rosalee said. She entered her room, quickly closed her door, and stood before her trunks. She almost regretted having packed so much. If she needed to leave quickly, she'd never be able to take everything with her. Not without someone to help carry it. It had only been by chance that she'd been fortunate enough to disembark, find a boarding house, and get her trunks taken there in such a short period of time.

Rosalee sat on the bed and dropped her head into her hands. What was she going to do? This was not a long-term solution. It was only a matter of time before her father found her. Not to mention, she'd foolishly told Mrs. Harper that she was a single woman seeking employment and her way in the world. For nearly five minutes straight, the woman had gone on and on about her unmarried nephew, the unmarried baker, and the unmarried blacksmith.

Even now, the memory upset her. If she'd wanted to be married, she'd be on that stage right now headed to the train, preparing herself to marry a man far, far older than her.

Luckily, Rosalee had plenty of practice having unwelcome conversations. She'd smiled and made all the right comments that, she hoped, were noncommittal. However, she sensed the boarding house owner might be a bit of a busybody, and that might not be the last she heard of the unmarried men around. It might not also be the last she heard about where she might seek employment—the diner, the dressmaker, as a nanny—which was tied for being the last thing she wanted.

Working somewhere would make her even more visible. It also wasn't something she was sure she could do. Rosalee had never cooked nor cleaned. She'd never worked in a store or restaurant or anywhere at all, for that matter. That wasn't to say she was helpless. She wasn't. But the skills she had, primarily organization and party planning, were unlikely to be things that were needed here.

So, she wasn't quite sure just how she was going to avoid that as well. Money wasn't a problem. Yet. Rosalee had enough to pay for the boarding house for a month, longer if she contacted the bank. But that wasn't something she wanted to do. Neither live here that long, in a room a third the size of her old one, nor contact the bank and lead her father to her.

So, what was she to do? Rosalee rubbed her temples. She hadn't thought this through at all. Perhaps the best thing to do would be to act as though she'd missed the stage, and find out when the next one was. Yes. That was actually a good idea. Her father would understand if she had accidently missed her connection and was a day or so behind. Surely there would be another in the next day or two.

Quickly, Rosalee stood and left her rented room. As she walked down the stairs, Mrs. Harper was giving a man a quick tour of the house. He must have been a new boarder too. She had been surprised at first that the woman kept both male and female boarders, but the men were kept on the first floor, and she only accepted two at a time, whereas she had up to six women.

Rosalee figured that was all right. The men, being on the first level, could help keep them safe if needed. But if they were to get out of hand, the six women boarders and the housekeeper should be more than enough to hold their own.

As Mrs. Harper and the man went through a doorway, Rosalee caught a glimpse of him and frowned. The man looked familiar, though she couldn't place where she'd seen him. It was a foolish notion, though. She didn't know anyone here in Cottonwood Falls. That was why she'd chosen the place.

Pushing the uneasy feeling from her mind, Rosalee left the boarding house and headed back to where she'd been not an hour before. Soon, she was standing in front of the stagecoach station, hands on her hips as she waited for the window to open. A small handwritten sign declared it to be closed for fifteen minutes. However, the person who'd put the sign up hadn't said when that time would start or end.

Without any other option, she stood waiting, feeling very exposed. It wasn't that anyone tried to talk to her. No, they passed her as though she didn't exist, which was fine with Rosalee. Yet, there was this prickle on the back of her neck that made her feel as though someone were watching her.

However, each time she turned around, Rosalee didn't see anyone close by or anything that seemed out of the ordinary.

"I'm just feeling paranoid, with all of what's happened," she muttered, then looked again, impatiently, at the station's window, hoping it would reopen.

Finally, after what was at least a half hour, the small curtains pulled over, the ticket window opened, and a wizened man with only a few hairs on his head stared at her. "Help you?" he asked.

"Yes. I was wondering when the next stage to Almeda came through," Rosalee said, giving him her best smile. "I need to take a train there East, but had to delay a few days."

"Well now," the man told her, consulting a large map on the wall. "That won't be for another week. Don't come through here but on Thursdays."

A week. Rosalee bit her lip in thought, then nodded and thanked the man, moving aside as another customer approached the window. Well, a week wasn't too bad. She'd just take the next stage, and find out the details of it in a few days. There would be somewhere to send a message to her aunt, so she'd do that tomorrow once she found out where. Waiting till tomorrow would also give her time to think about what she wanted to say.

She started slowly toward the boarding house, not in any rush to be back in the cramped room. As she passed by a store, she glanced over to see a woman, not much older than herself, being helped into a wagon by a man many years her senior. He climbed up himself, with a great deal of effort, then leaned over and kissed her cheek with a loud smacking sound.

The action repulsed Rosalee, though she knew it shouldn't. Why, for all she knew, that was a father and daughter, but all she could see was herself, and the man she was to marry. A shudder went through her, and Rosalee wrapped her arms around herself.

She had to do something. Getting back on the stagecoach wasn't an option. So, what was? In truth, Rosalee had no idea. She'd never been alone before. She wasn't quite sure how to take care of herself.

Maybe I should inquire about the stage going elsewhere, she mused. *Somewhere where I can't be found.*

But then that led back to the issue of money. She'd need to work eventually. Sooner than that, if she were to make her funds stretch. But what could she do? Just as Rosalee decided to look for a newspaper for sale, that strange prickling on her neck happened, and she twisted her head just in time to catch sight of a man disappearing into a building.

Rosalee's pulse quickened, and her feet carried her swiftly to the boarding house. The situation was worse than she thought. Not only had she made a terrible mistake by getting off the stage, but someone was following her.

Did this person know her father was wealthy? Or was he simply preying on her, as a woman traveling alone?

She'd been so stupid, getting off the stage in a small town. She should have waited until someone else—another woman—had gotten off, and asked her for advice on what to do.

Rosalee wrapped her arms around herself and shivered. Wonderful. What a fine mess this was. She was likely going to be kidnapped or killed, in a town where no one would find her or knew her. All because she was trying to escape an unwanted marriage.

Rosalee wasn't sure who she was more furious with. Herself, for her own role in this, or her father, for being the cause of all her troubles.

Chapter 6

Aaron scowled as Rosalee slowly walked down the sidewalk. It made it incredibly hard to follow someone when they poked along at a snail's pace like she was. If he got too close, then she'd see him. If he stood back too far, well, he might lose her. Though that wasn't likely given the pace she was walking now, Aaron had the feeling she suspected she was being followed, due to her speeding up and then slowing down strategically at glass windows, where she'd study them for a maddeningly long time.

"Hurry up, won't you?" he growled, half wishing she'd hear him. Better yet, he wished she'd just stay in the boarding house. There, it was much easier to keep an eye on her. As the men had rooms on the lower level, and he was fortunate his was close to the front door, he was able to keep his room's door open a crack to watch who came in and went out. His window gave him a nice view too.

So far, they'd been there in Cottonwood Falls for three long, exhausting, worrying, stressful days. He didn't know why the woman was here. She wasn't doing anything, and she didn't seem to be enjoying herself. Should he confront her? Tell her she was getting on that next stage no matter what? This wasn't her final destination, and it most definitely wasn't his.

But each time he thought about approaching her, something made him stop. He wasn't sure what. He was stuck here in this small town until she made her move. Hopefully, that would be soon.

And since he had to keep a close watch on her, Aaron had to take his meals with the other boarders, which included Rosalee. She stayed quiet, usually looking down at her plate, and he did the same. So far, she hadn't recognized him from the stage. As for talking...the boarding house owner did enough talking for the whole lot of them there.

He supposed Mrs. Harper was nice enough, but there was no mistaking she was nosey too. He'd invented a story about going out to visit family, but being told they had the fever, so he'd decided to wait here in town until it passed, on account of him not wanting to catch it. A plausible story, and one that he made sure to mention when he went to the post office "looking" for a message.

The boarding house owner had clucked her sorrow, and in her next breath asked if he was married and if he was planning to be, because she knew a nice young woman who worked at the general store. He'd answered he wasn't married, but he also wasn't looking.

"You will be," Mrs. Harper said with a chuckle. "I can see romance in your future."

Aaron doubted that. He wondered if she'd said the same to Rosalee. Though, he didn't see romance in her future once he got her on that train headed East. He saw frustration and unhappiness.

And, maybe, just on occasion, he felt a twinge of guilt when he thought about that. So far, he hadn't seen a bad side of Rosalee. But she was likely hiding it, like her father did so well, and deserved whatever ill thing she got.

He bent over to tie his shoe when he saw Rosalee stop again, this time at the dressmaker's window. Yep. She was on to him. She might be facing the window, but he could tell by the tiny movements of her head that her eyes were searching behind her. This had been what they did for the last few days. She walked through the town, and he followed her, trying not to be spotted. It was exhausting. Possibly even more difficult than the jobs her father had him doing back at his place.

What was she doing? Aaron didn't understand why she was here and why she was walking around. What had made her willfully get off the stage? She had to have had a reason.

He stiffened. Had her father told her to do it as a test to see if he was going to get her back East? He wouldn't put it past the man. But, Rosalee didn't seem like the kind of woman to like or appreciate being inconvenienced, which was what this was. For her and for him.

Aaron started to run his fingers through his hair, but remembered his hat was on and jammed low over his face. Darned woman. Had him so flustered he couldn't even remember if he was wearing a hat or not!

He wanted to give up, but there was too much at stake. His future. Which was why he was hoping she'd had a change of heart and would be getting on the next stage to take her to the train station. He knew she'd asked about it. He'd been listening in. But she hadn't said more than a thank you, so he wasn't sure if that meant she was going or not.

Aaron's fingers itched to get that paper from Rosalee's father, saying that he was a free man. That no debt was owed. But he wouldn't get it until the woman was on that train and delivered to her aunt. He ground his teeth in frustration. She was so infuriating! No wonder she wasn't married before now.

Rosalee started walking again, and turned the corner of a building. Aaron sped up. He couldn't see where she went. He thought she'd turned right, but as he walked past the opening between the barber and the shoemaker, he didn't see her in the narrow alley, only a pile of crates.

"Where'd she go?" Aaron's head darted side to side, and he stepped back out into the street again. He couldn't see her. He moved back into the alleyway. Maybe she'd cut through all the way and headed to the back of the buildings. He wasn't sure why she would, but there wasn't anywhere else to go.

Hurriedly, he focused on the small opening between the buildings about fifteen paces away. He strode toward it, his fast walk becoming a slow jog, then a faster one. He came to the exit and looked left. She wasn't there. He turned toward the right, and something hard swung right at him, sending Aaron stumbling backward, his shoulder striking the building.

Chapter 7

Rosalee's neck didn't stop prickling. The feeling had nagged at her from the time she left the boarding house until...well, it hadn't stopped. At all. For three days. Truthfully, the last three days had been miserable. There was nothing at all to do in this tiny town. At least, not when one was having to hide. She couldn't browse endlessly in the stores. First, that would make people remember her. Second, she might see something she wanted, and Rosalee had neither an endless supply of money nor the desire to leave those items behind, with the others she couldn't take if she had to leave suddenly.

She slowed, stopping to study a shop window. Only, she wasn't really window shopping. She was trying to get a glimpse of whatever it was making the hairs on her neck stand up and her chest tight. She scanned the reflection.

Again, she saw no one. Either this was all her imagination, or else the person was very good at what they were doing.

But who was it? Had her father perhaps already sent someone after her? Or had they been there from the start to be sure she got to her aunt? But that meant it was someone who'd been on the stage with her. So, who? Rosalee tried to remember each person she'd ridden with. She couldn't dismiss any of them as a potential suspect. But the issue was that she had been so lost in a fog of despair, she hadn't really noticed anyone there, except for the small glimpse of the handsome man who had been sitting across from her holding a newspaper. When he'd drifted off, her eyes had unashamedly roamed over him in a most unladylike way.

But she didn't care. She'd be a married woman soon. This might be her last chance to admire someone who looked kind. Like the sort of man who would treat his wife well. She wasn't sure the man she was going to marry would be that way. With his age, he likely only wanted her to make him feel young and had no interest in what she wanted. There was nothing wrong with growing older, Rosalee had reflected. But the refusal to admit that one was, was where the problem lay.

With a small sigh, Rosalee walked a few more steps to the dressmaker and studied the simply cut moss-green dress on display. The sleeves had embroidered leaves on them. It was pretty. Understated. It would suit someone in the town nicely, she was sure. Rosalee had just turned when the flash of someone ducking around the side of a building caught her attention.

Her heart sped up. She was being followed. And now she knew by whom. A man! Just...who was he? The hat on his head covered his face. And why was he following her? Rosalee walked briskly. She had to lose him. She couldn't go seeking help. That might send her father right to her. No, she had to take care of this on her own.

Between the next two buildings was a long alleyway. Rosalee turned into it, then raised her skirts and ran as fast as she could. Nearly panting from the exertion, she waited around the far corner. She could hear someone in the alley. They were muttering to themselves. Then, the person's voice grew louder. They were heading toward her.

A loose curl struck Rosalee's cheek as she frantically looked side to side for a place to hide or something to defend herself with. Her eyes fell on a discarded stick. It wasn't much, but it was stout, and it was something—which was better than nothing.

Rosalee pulled the stick to her shoulder, and as the person rounded the corner, she swung with all her might. The stick snapped into pieces across his arm and chest, but it was enough to stop the man, send him staggering backward.

He shook his head and then steadied himself. The stranger fixed his eyes on her, and an incredulous expression came over his face. "What'd you do that for?" he asked.

She straightened her shoulders and tossed back her head. The irritating curl smacked her in the face again. "Why are you following me?" she asked, balling her hands into fists. The gesture was less to be intimidating, and more to hide her trembling hands. Rosalee had no intention of acting afraid.

The man studied her for a moment, then shrugged and put his hands in his pockets. "What the heck. Might as well tell you."

"I'm listening," she answered coolly.

"Your father told me to make sure you got on the train East," he said. A smile came over his face. "Even if it was kicking and screaming."

She tensed. There was no doubt he was telling the truth. "You wouldn't."

"Try me," he said. "Since you know I've been following you, there's no point in hiding or trying to be subtle about it."

"You're the man from the stagecoach," she suddenly gasped. Her cheeks colored. He was the handsome man she'd been staring at.

"Is that the first time you've ever seen me?" he asked her, a smirk on his lips.

Rosalee's lips frowned slightly, and she shrugged. "Have we met?" There. That should shame him into politeness.

"Not as such," he answered. The man leaned against the building's wall and crossed his arms. "So, now that you know I'm here, it will make it that much easier when you get on the next stage to get to the train. You won't be asking questions."

"That's where you are wrong," Rosalee said calmly. "I won't be getting on the stage or the train. I'm not going East."

He shot up from the wall. "Yes, you are. I'm going to see you do."

"No, I'm not. Do you have a problem with your hearing?" Rosalee snapped. Her eyes narrowed. "How do you know me?"

"I've seen you around." He shrugged. "Been living on your father's property and working for him for a few months now."

Rosalee studied him. "I don't recall seeing you," she finally said. It wasn't quite true, but he didn't need to know that. She might have noticed him here and there, but not enough to remember. In fact, she hadn't recognized him on the stage at all, even though she'd been staring at him. Rosalee knew why that was, too. Her mother didn't allow her to wear the spectacles that she needed for distance seeing.

"That doesn't surprise me. You wouldn't, would you, princess? I'm not worthy of the likes of you, am I? Aaron Woods, at your service." He gave her a mock bow.

Rosalee took a half step back in shock. She didn't understand why someone she'd never met before was being so cold to her. So nasty. What was wrong with him? It was on the tip of her tongue to mention that wasn't why, but she decided he didn't need any explanations from her. She pressed her lips together. "Go away," she said firmly.

"I can't," the man answered. He took a step closer.

"You can," she said. "How much do you want? Fifty dollars? Pretend you never saw me. That should be enough."

The man stopped, and his upper lip curled. "You think you can buy me? You're just like your father, thinking that because you're rich you can do whatever you want."

"How dare you?" Rosalee gasped. "You don't know me and you don't know my father."

"That's where you're wrong," he snarled. "I know plenty about him. Know how he ruined my life, and that getting you on that train is my only chance to get it back."

Rosalee backed further away. She didn't understand what he meant, but the man was obviously crazy. She regretted being here behind the buildings where there was no one around to help her. If she screamed, would anyone even hear her?

He took another step closer to her.

"I won't go," she said, holding her ground. "No one will make me."

"Look," the man sighed, stopping. "I'm not going to hurt you. I just want you to get on the stage and then the train. Go East. Get to your aunt. Get ma—do whatever it is you're supposed to do."

She shook her head slowly. "You don't understand why I can't," she said. "Why I won't."

He shrugged. "No, I don't. I don't really care either, but if it will get you packed up and gone sooner, like a good little girl, then tell me. I'll pretend to care."

Rosalee took another step backward, then another. He was making her angry. The absolute loathing toward her in his voice upset her. Why was he like this? What had she done to him? Well, other than hit him with a stick, but he had been following her, and she didn't know why at the time. She had no regrets on her end. In fact, she wished there had been a larger, stouter stick nearby.

Pressing her lips together, she raised her chin. "I don't owe you any explanations," she said, turning and running for the boarding house, skirts raised above her ankles.

Chapter 8

Aaron's shoulder stung where Rosalee had struck him with the stick. Honestly, he didn't know she'd had that much strength in her. The woman had sure caught him by surprise. But, he also hadn't missed that split-second expression on her face as she'd swung at him with every bit of determination she could muster.

Fear.

She had been scared. Of him.

Was it because he'd been following her? Or were his words, filled with anger about her father and his situation, the cause and he was misremembering when he saw that expression? Aaron wasn't sure. Maybe it was both.

He didn't want her to look at him that way. In all the times he'd seen her from a distance, and the rare time he'd seen her smile, he'd always imagined what it would feel like if that smile was for him. What sweet words might fall from her lips. He'd secretly hoped more than once she'd approach him so he could talk to her, even if it was just a moment. But she never had, and he'd found himself thinking about her far more than he should have.

And then, every single time, he'd hated himself for his thoughts and dreams. Disliked her, for the kind of man her father was and what he'd done to him, how he'd stolen away his life, ruined his reputation.

But fear...no, that was never his intention. He'd never wanted her to feel fear from him.

That loathsome whisper of guilt welled up in Aaron, and he pushed it to the side. She didn't need to be scared of him. It wasn't his intention to hurt her. Anyway, the woman had plenty of gumption that he saw.

And plenty of something else. He just wasn't sure what. He didn't intend to apologize, though. She needed to do what she was supposed to do, and get on that train. The sooner she was away from him, and his thoughts that wanted to protect her and keep her safe, right there with him, the better.

Maybe he'd been a little rude. Aggressive, just now. But he'd felt hurt that she hadn't recognized him. That she hadn't recalled seeing him at her father's place when he knew she'd looked at him many times. His pride was stung, and disappointment came over him.

He sighed as he walked toward the boarding house. He'd seen her flee in that direction, and watched as she went inside. So, he could take his time. She wasn't going anywhere. Of that, he was sure. Wasn't sure of much else right now, but of that he was.

This was a complicated situation. For him, for her...and from what he'd observed, Rosalee didn't deserve the unkind thoughts he'd had toward her.

He rubbed at his shoulder. The stick had been a little thicker than his thumb. There might be a bruise tomorrow, but he'd had worse. Given it, too. Just never by a woman. What had made her react in that way?

Why, he thought if a woman felt threatened she'd scream for help or hide. Not lure her pursuer into a trap and hit him with something! Her behavior puzzled him.

And then, there was her absolute insistence she wasn't getting on the train. Why, she'd even tried to pay him to pretend he hadn't seen her! It was obvious she wasn't wanting to go. So, why had she gotten on the stage in the first place?

Aaron rubbed at the back of his head as he walked up the steps to the boarding house. Maybe she'd learned her father was marrying her off and she didn't like the guy. Not that he cared about that any. No, what he cared about was getting her on that stage and getting on the train. That was important. Nothing else was. Not what she wanted, not what he secretly longed for.

But how was he going to do that? It was obvious that she was going to be a little more difficult than he'd imagined.

Aaron paused as he passed the general store, and decided to go inside. Just a moment wouldn't hurt. He didn't think Rosalee would leave the boarding house, and he'd be able to see her if she did, the windows of the store were so plentiful.

As he pushed open the door, another man looked up. Aaron recognized him as the doctor who'd greeted him when he first arrived.

"Hello," Dr. Mason said. "Settling in?"

"Yes," Aaron said. "Cottonwood Falls is a nice town. Though, we won't be staying too long."

"That's a shame," the doctor said. Aaron noticed his arms full of books. "We love when someone passing by decides to call this town home."

Aaron rubbed at his head. "Well, you know how some things are," he said, trying to figure out how to both end the conversation and not explain the situation, "got to do what the woman wants."

The doctor laughed and headed toward the door. "Well, I can't fault a man for wanting his wife to be happy. Have a good afternoon."

Wife.

The word jingled in the air, just like the small bell over the shop door had. Aaron liked the sound of it, yet at the same time, the idea terrified him. He couldn't imagine being married to someone like Rosalee. She was so beautiful and delicate, so intelligent and sharp, so independent and strong. Not the type to want to settle, especially with a man like him.

Aaron swallowed hard, and glanced toward the boarding house. He knew where her window was, and saw the curtain move. She was likely looking out at the town. Looking for him? He wasn't sure.

Continuing around the store, Aaron got some shaving soap, and a handful of peppermints. He paused at the dime novels, and then decided to get one. It had been hard to fall asleep at night. Maybe a little reading would help.

After paying, Aaron headed back toward the boarding house. He debated stopping for a time on the porch, sitting in one of the chairs and trying to relax, but he knew the kitchen door exited where he wouldn't be able to see if Rosalee left. So, inside he went, intending to go to his usual spot and watch over her.

She might not like it, but he'd promised to see no harm came to her. Even in a small town like this, where likely very little happened, Aaron was determined to follow through on that.

And if that meant he had to look at her lovely face all the more, he couldn't say he minded. Rosalee Milton was—

Someone he had to stop thinking about.

Chapter 9

After confronting the man following her around town, Rosalee was nearly breathless by the time she'd reached the boarding house. Of course, Mrs. Harper had stopped her the moment she walked in. She hadn't been surprised. The woman seemed to thrive on knowing the goings-on of everything and everyone in town, but Rosalee softened a little when the older woman approached her, concern etched into the wrinkles on her face.

"Have you a moment?" Mrs. Harper asked. Her hands were twisting in her apron. "In private?"

"Oh," Rosalee answered, surprise washing over her. She wasn't sure what had distressed the other woman, but was certain it was nothing she'd done, so didn't let herself feel unsettled. "Of course. Where should we go?"

"How about the kitchen?" the older woman asked. "I can pour us some tea."

Rosalee followed Mrs. Harper into the kitchen. She shouldn't have been staring, but she was, and also feeling slightly out of place. Rosalee could count on perhaps just her fingers and toes the number of times that she'd been in a kitchen. Usually, Cook came to her mother's study with concerns or to discuss menus. The odd time Rosalee wanted something outside of mealtimes, she'd ring for it.

The kitchen looked...cozy. Rag rugs covered the floor in spots where it looked someone would stand for long periods of time, something was bubbling in a large pot atop the cast-iron stove, and smells of cinnamon and something bread-y filled her nose.

"It smells wonderful in here," Rosalee said, taking a seat at the small table.

The boarding house owner set down two cups of tea and a plate with cookies. "That'll be these cookies," Mrs. Harper said. "My grandmother's recipe."

Rosalee bit into one. It nearly melted on her tongue. "This might be the best cookie I've ever eaten," she sighed happily.

The other woman flushed, and then smiled proudly. "Everyone loved Grammy's recipe. I'm pleased I can do right by it."

Nodding in agreement, Rosalee took a sip of her tea. "Forgive me for saying so, but you look concerned about something," she said.

"It's because I am." The other woman clasped her hands before her. "I wanted to talk to you, before I turned out that Mr. Woods on his ear."

That caught Rosalee's attention. On the one hand, if he was forced to leave the boarding house, that might solve her problem of him trying to drag her back. On the other, as much as she didn't care for the fact that he was working for her father, it wouldn't be right of her to stand by and watch as he was removed from his lodgings, perhaps unfairly. Especially if it had something to do with her.

Rosalee had a sinking suspicion, based on his behavior, that there was far more to the story than she realized.

When Mrs. Harper didn't say anything else, Rosalee asked, "What of him?"

"I've seen him following you," the woman said bluntly. "And it's concerning me. A young woman, all alone, and a man following her."

"Ahh." Rosalee wasn't sure how to answer that, so she took another sip of her tea, and hoped something would come to her mind quickly.

"Now, before I make my decision, I just wanted to know. Is he an unwanted suitor? Or are you playing hard to get?"

Rosalee choked. For nearly a minute, she coughed, trying to catch her breath. Mrs. Harper had jumped up and thumped her on the back several times before Rosalee held up a hand and regained control of herself.

"Mrs. Harper," Rosalee said, "I'm not playing hard to get. I'm not interested in a relationship with anyone."

"I see." The older woman frowned. "So, he's pursuing you, unwanted."

"No, that's not it either," Rosalee sighed, as the truth slipped out before she could stop it. "He and I know each other. Not directly acquaintanced, but he works for my father. He was sent to...protect me. See that I got to where I was meant to go."

"But you are here," the boarding house owner said. "Is this where you were meant to be?"

"Not exactly," Rosalee said, fighting the urge to squirm like a child.

The other woman's brows rose. "And where are you supposed to be?"

She sighed. "Back East, with my aunt. Getting married to a man my father chose."

"I see." Mrs. Harper sat back in her chair. "And I take it that isn't something you wanted to have happen."

"No, it's not," Rosalee said softly, letting her forefinger trail over the tablecloth. Taking a deep breath, she looked up. "I know you won't understand, but—"

"Not understand?" Mrs. Harper's voice rose. "Not understand a man telling you how to live your life without letting you have any say in something so serious? Oh, I do, my girl." She shook her head. "My father did the same. Married me off to a terrible man. Wouldn't let me be with the one I longed for."

The past came over Mrs. Harper's face, and Rosalee found herself leaning forward, as if that would help her hear the story any better. "What happened?" she asked. Perhaps if the woman before her had been given a happy ending, she could have one herself.

Mrs. Harper's chin wobbled. "My Freddy, the man I loved, waited for me. Waited twenty years. When my first husband passed away, we got married. All those years wasted didn't matter to him. He said he'd wait forever, just to spend a day with me." She wiped at her eyes. "But the Lord only let us have a few years of happiness together before he took him home."

"I'm so sorry," Rosalee said, reaching over to gently squeeze the other woman's hand.

"No need to be," the boarding house owner sniffled. "We had time together. And we started this place together." She looked around the kitchen fondly. "I still feel him here with me. Was he who thought we'd make a good business of it. And we have. We wanted others to feel at home."

"You've succeeded. I've felt very welcome," Rosalee said. "And taken care of."

They were both silent. Rosalee was lost in her thoughts, and wondered if Mrs. Harper was too. Finally, she said, "I wish I did have someone I loved. That, at least, would be an excuse for not getting married. But the truth is, I don't. I never wanted to get married," she said honestly. "I enjoy travel. My father had enough money I could do what I wanted, go where I liked. But..." she shook her head, "but I'm scared. I don't want to marry that man, but I've no other options. I don't think I can provide for myself. I've also no other options for marriage."

"If only I knew a way to help," Mrs. Harper said, "but that's something you'll need to figure out." She smiled then, and her voice lowered, "But you are wrong, about not having another option for marriage."

"Ah, yes. This morning, you mentioned the tailor's son, the pigman, and the tinsmith, didn't you?" Rosalee said, trying not to grimace.

Mrs. Harper waved her hand dismissively. "Not for you. They aren't good enough. I meant Mr. Woods."

Rosalee's eyes widened, but before she could speak, Mrs. Harper continued. "I see how he looks at you."

She laughed then, in amusement. After the way the man had spoken to her earlier, she didn't think he felt anything but disgust and anger toward her. "I told you. He's just here to see I get East. That's it. There's nothing romantic in the makings."

"I don't know," the older woman said, raising an eyebrow.

"I do," Rosalee assured.

"I'm glad that's all settled, then," Mrs. Harper said. "I feel much better knowing that Mr. Woods is here to see you to your destination."

"Yes," Rosalee said, and rose from her seat. "Thank you for the tea, Mrs. Harper. I'm going to go rest for a little, but I do appreciate you looking after me." She paused then, as a realization came over her. "Oddly enough, I don't think anyone has ever done that before, and it's very kind of you."

The older woman shrugged. "Just being a decent human being," she said. "But as I said, I think Mr. Woods is looking at you. Like it or not."

"Not," Rosalee said sarcastically.

Mrs. Harper laughed. "Maybe not, but you know, there's something nice feeling about a man looking both at and after you."

Rosalee just smiled and shook her head as she left the kitchen. Perhaps so, but she wasn't so sure Mr. Woods was the one for that. He really did seem to dislike her. If he'd had even the least bit of interest in her, he wouldn't have been so cold or cruel in the way he spoke to her.

Now that Mrs. Harper knew why she was there, and that Mr. Woods was not only connected to her father but knew she had no desire to get on the train, Rosalee realized she was at a crossroads. There were three choices before her.

Go East and accept her fate, wait for her father to arrive and drag her there, or get Mr. Woods on her side. He hadn't wanted to be paid to leave her alone, so perhaps there was something else that she could do to convince him that it would be better if he forgot all about her and just went wherever it was he was headed. But what might that be?

Rosalee wasn't sure, but she was determined to figure it out.

Chapter 10

After he pushed open the heavy oak door of the boarding house, Aaron was greeted by both the smell of freshly baked bread, a warm and yeasty goodness that made his mouth water, and Mrs. Harper.

She smiled brightly when she saw him. "Mr. Woods! A fine afternoon, isn't it?" she greeted him.

"Ma'am," he said, nodding at her. Hopefully that was all he'd need to say and she'd leave him alone.

"You know, Mr. Woods," the woman continued, a warning tone to her voice, "the way to win a woman's attention isn't to upset her. Or to follow her about town. Even if you might be trying to protect her."

Aaron had been mid-step to his room, and stumbled. "Ah, I'm not sure what you mean," he stammered.

The boarding house owner shook her finger at him, the smile on her face even larger. "Now, now. You can't fool me. I know a man interested in a woman when I see one. But, and I hope you don't mind my saying so, you are going about things all wrong, my dear boy. You'll never get a woman by slinking about like you have been. Even if it's your job to escort her to her final destination."

He swallowed hard. Maybe he hadn't been as stealthy as he'd thought he was. Or maybe it was just the boarding house owner was too nosey for anyone's good. How did she know what she was hinting at? "I'm—"

"Needing to do the grand gestures a woman wants!" Mrs. Harper said, throwing her arms wide. "Why, a woman like Miss Milton, she's *special*. She could have anyone that she wants. Have you seen how lovely and cultured she is? A far better stock than most."

Aaron shook his head. "You seem to be misunderstanding the situation. I'm not interested in Miss Milton—or anyone else."

She laughed, and reached over to pat his shoulder. "You keep telling yourself that. She was trying to convince herself of that too."

"What?" Aaron stared at her, confused. "When?" But as she just continued to smile, he growled, "I'm not telling myself anything. I'm not looking for a relationship."

But his reaction didn't make Mrs. Harper stop. She clasped her hands together and grew thoughtful in her expression. Nodding slowly, she started to tick off on her fingers. "Flowers are a good start. A picnic. Perhaps you could offer to take her on a walk." Her face was hopeful. Aaron wasn't sure why. Did the woman just like to see romance everywhere she turned? She had been asking a lot of questions when he first came.

"Mrs. Harper," he said, trying to suppress a sigh, "I appreciate the suggestions. When the time comes where I want to court a woman, I'll be sure to use those. In the meantime, I'm not interested in Rosalee. Not at all. Matter of fact, I don't even like her."

"Rosalee, eh? Does she know you call her by her first name?"

The smug look on the boarding house owner's face was a little too much for him. Luckily for them both, someone else walked in just then, inquiring about a room, and Aaron managed to keep his mouth shut before he said something hurtful or spiteful.

Their conversation, though brief, had just added fuel to the fire he'd been feeling. He wasn't interested in Rosalee at all. She was a job. A means to an end. Nothing more. At all.

And as the rest of the evening unfolded, with dinner all together, reading the newspaper in the parlor, and keeping an eye on whether Rosalee went out until Mrs. Harper locked the boarding house for the night, that's just what Aaron kept repeating to himself.

But he hadn't done a good enough job convincing himself it was true, because late that night, he tossed and turned, and couldn't get Rosalee's face out of his mind.

That evening at dinner, she'd been quiet, as usual. But there was a sadness in her eyes, a heartache on her face, and it pricked his conscience in a way he didn't like at all. Made him wonder, even feel sorry for the women in the world who were traded off at the whim of another. What would their lives be like? What would happen to Rosalee?

She was beautiful, but beyond that she was also a lot more than he'd seen at first glance. Though he'd had a lot more glances than just one since he'd first laid eyes on her. A part of him wanted to get to know more, see who she really was beneath the cool exterior she wore. Aaron was starting to suspect she might be more complex than he realized. Maybe those fancy dresses and hats she wore were a type of armor, shielding her from the world. Did women do that? It wasn't really a foolish idea.

However, maybe he was a fool for wasting time thinking about her.

***

Aaron peered through the crack in his door. If he angled himself just so, he could see Rosalee in the sitting room. She was by herself, reading a book. At least, it appeared that she was. He suspected she wasn't, though, due to the fact she hadn't turned any pages since she sat down.

"You can stop staring at me," she said, her gaze directed toward him.

Surprised, Aaron stepped back. Then, he opened the door a little more. "Just doing my job," he said.

"Your job wasn't to watch me," she said dryly. "It was to get me back East."

"Maybe I'm working on the plan for that," he told her, crossing his arms and leaning against the wall.

"You've got to stop spying on me," Rosalee said, closing the book and setting it in her lap. "Mrs. Harper thinks you like me!"

"Couldn't be further from the truth," he promised, as he stepped closer. "But yes, she does. Told me a bunch of ways women like to be flattered and suggested I try them on you."

Rosalee arched one of her perfect brows. "Such as?"

He shrugged. "Flowers. Picnics. That sort of thing."

To his surprise, a wistful expression flashed across her face, before the cool look he was used to seeing took its proper place.

"I wouldn't know," she said.

He narrowed his eyes. "A beautiful woman like you? I'm sure men are falling all over themselves to get your attention."

"Not mine," she said with a small shake of her head. "My father's." She studied him for a moment. "I'd...like to talk with you. Could we go for a walk?"

Caught off guard, Aaron nodded before he could think better of it. He watched as Rosalee set the book back on the small shelf, and headed to the boarding house door. She paused and glanced over her shoulder. "Are you coming?"

"After you, princess," he said, with an exaggerated bow.

She scoffed, but went outside. Aaron fell into step with her, and they walked in silence for a time. Finally, without warning, Rosalee stopped and faced him. "Mr. Woods—"

"Aaron," he told her. "And I'm calling you Rosalee."

She raised her brow again, but nodded. "Very well. Though, I can count on one hand the number of men who call me by my first name."

He just shrugged. Let her mull over that. To his surprise, she didn't seem bothered.

"Mr—Aaron, I want to make something clear. I'm not going back home or East to my aunt." When Aaron started to say something, she held up a hand. "Let me finish," she said. "Give me that much."

Aaron nodded, his eyes lingering on her long, slim fingers. Her hands looked soft. As though she'd never worked a day in her life. Probably hadn't. He wondered if the rest of her was that soft. If he reached out and touched her cheek—

He stiffened. What was he doing, thinking like that? He glanced away, but when he looked back, he realized she'd been talking, and he'd missed all of what she'd said.

"I'm sorry," he said. "Will you say that again?"

She stamped her foot. "You are infuriating! Were you not listening, or do you just like to hear me talk?"

He smirked. "Both."

Her cheeks colored a soft pink. Then she took a deep breath. "I'm asking for a head start."

"For what?"

"To run. To hide. Get away. Start over." Rosalee plucked at her sleeve. "I can't marry the man my father has sold me to." At his surprised look, she continued, "Because that's what it is. His business deal is contingent upon our marriage. But I refuse to marry a man more than a decade older than my father."

"Older than..." Aaron shook his head as though it would clear his ears. Had he heard wrong? No wonder she didn't want to go East. He didn't blame her one bit. The idea of Rosalee marrying someone more than twice her age made him shudder, so he could only imagine how she felt. She'd be more than just on the man's arm. He'd expect kisses. To hold her. To...

It was vile to think about, especially when Rosalee wasn't willing whatsoever. He wondered for a moment just how many women had been in that sort of a situation, and been without any option but to marry who they were told to, even if they could have been older than their father.

Aaron felt badly for her, he did. But the fact of the matter was, he couldn't do it. Besides, her idea of a head start wouldn't work. Not if her father tried to track her down.

"I assume you've already told my father I'm here," she said grimly. "So I might only have hours. But, I'm begging you to be decent, and do the right thing."

Aaron sighed, and jammed his hands into his pockets. "I can't," he said quietly.

Her voice was cold. "Is it because he's paid you well?"

"No." He shook his head. "It's because your father is a—"

Aaron wasn't sure what made him stop. Made him hold in the words he wanted to say. He looked away, torn between a desperate feeling brewing inside him and the smallest bit of compassion he had for Rosalee.

A touch brought him out of his thoughts, and he glanced down to see her small hand on his arm. "Tell me," she commanded, her strong voice a complete contrast to her gentle touch.

"It's not polite," he admitted. "And it wouldn't be right of me to say such things about your father."

She smiled, just a small upturn of the corners on her lips, but something about it brought her eyes to life. "It's likely nothing I've not heard. Or thought."

He laughed at that. "I doubt it."

Her hands went to her hips. "Try me."

"All right," he said, accepting her challenge. "Your father isn't a nice man. He's a liar. Greedy. Does things for his own benefit."

She shrugged. "I'm inclined to agree. Did you forget, he's arranged for me to become the wife of someone in exchange for a business merger?"

"He ruins lives," Aaron said, staring off into the distance.

"I know that too," she said. "Look at mine. It's in shambles right now."

He shook his head. "No, princess. Yours isn't ruined. You still have a chance. You might have less freedom, but you still have some. Unlike me."

She was quiet, then said, "Please don't call me princess. Father used to, and back then it felt special. But now, the word makes me feel trapped. A princess in a tower with no escape."

He gave the smallest of nods. "As you wish."

After a few breaths of silence, she asked, "What do you mean, you don't have freedom?"

Aaron swallowed hard. Somehow, and he wasn't sure when, he'd started to lose some of that dislike for Rosalee. It had been replaced with admiration. Even if what she wanted was futile. There was no escape from a man like her father. She just didn't know it yet.

When he realized she was still staring at him, Aaron said, "You know I work for your father?" At her nod, he continued, "It wasn't by choice."

"Then why don't you leave?"

"I'm trapped there," he said, his voice low. "Because of your father. If I run, he'll see me locked up. At a minimum. But if I get you on that train East, I get my freedom again. The freedom that he stole."

The startled look on her face should have made him feel gratified. Instead, Aaron felt pity. "You don't know the things he does to others, do you?" he asked.

"I'm starting to have an idea," Rosalee answered, walking the short distance to a bench. She situated herself, and patted the empty seat next to her.

Aaron sat, careful not to be too close.

"Tell me everything," she told him, her voice low. "Even if you think it would be painful for me to hear."

"Are you sure?" Aaron asked.

She nodded.

Aaron closed his eyes for a moment. He could see it all perfectly. That day his life paused. Put him in a type of purgatory.

"I had a fledgling business," Aaron began. "Four mares and a stallion. I got wind of a fine mare, one of a breed that matched my stallion. That's rare," he added, "out here, unless you have one specially sent in. I went to look at it, the same time as another man. Your father."

He glanced at her, but she simply nodded.

"I was there, alone, looking the mare over. Had talked to the owner, and he was getting ready to come out to the barn with me, when your father came and they started talking. I'd made up my mind I wanted her. Had the cash money too, right in my pocket.

"But your father came into the barn just then. Told me the horse was his. I told him it wasn't, I'd gotten there first, and I was getting her. About that time, the owner walked in, and your father made up a story about how he'd seen me trying to steal the horse."

"How could the owner have thought that?" Rosalee asked. "Surely he'd have been suspicious."

"Sure, except for the owner happened to be a friend of his," Aaron said wryly. "Went right along with the story, and sold the horse to your father. The owner suggested that I give him my mares and stallion to make amends for attempted horse thievery. Was that or my neck."

At her shudder, he continued. "I didn't believe him. Laughed. Your father told me he'd show me how he always got what he wanted. Turned out the man selling the mare was a judge. He stood right there listening to your father tell me that I was going to give up my horses and come work for him to clear the debt of attempted horse theft. Or else." Aaron touched his throat. "I'm fond of living, so I said yes."

Rosalee shook her head. "I don't believe you."

"You don't have to, pr—Rosalee. But it's the truth."

She sat there quietly. Aaron didn't disturb her. He'd said a lot. Likely, she needed time to let it digest. Maybe she believed his story, maybe she didn't. Either way, it didn't matter.

"That's why I've got to get you back East," he finished.

"I don't understand," she told him. "Is that because of your debt? Father is insisting, since you work for him?"

"No," he said, leaning forward and dropping his head in his hands. He felt terrible telling her, and worse when her soft hand touched his.

"Tell me," she said.

"It's because once you're there, he'll erase my debt. I get my life back." Aaron looked at her then, and wondered if she could see the torment on his face. He felt bad saying it. Tried to soften the words.

"It's nothing against you, Rosalee. I just want my life back. To be free. Have my reputation clear and start over someplace. And I'm afraid I won't get that, unless I see you there."

"And to the marriage I'm trying to escape," she said quietly, her shoulders slumping.

"I'm sorry," Aaron whispered. "I wish it weren't like this. But it is. Only one of us gets to walk away."

Chapter 11

Rosalee sat in silence on the bench. She didn't know what to think after she heard Aaron's story. Her head was almost spinning in disbelief. She'd known that her father had been a little...forceful in his business dealings at times. But her parents had said that was simply the way of things. Nothing was meant by it.

However, seeing the pain in Aaron's eyes and hearing the hurt and anger in his voice had her questioning everything she thought that she knew about her parents. It wasn't right to completely upend someone's life, just for your personal gain. It was bad enough they were doing it to her, but it was almost expected, at her age. But to a stranger? How many others had her father done this to? To everyone who worked for him?

She remembered what her mother had said, about them being in financial difficulties. That was why the business deal was so important to her father. He wanted the company, at any cost.

Rosalee wondered if her parents even knew anything about the man they were wanting to marry her to. Was he kind? He was old, she knew that. But what if he was cruel? Expected her to act in ways she didn't feel comfortable? What if he was abusive?

Of course, he might be nice. Thoughtful. Attentive. But if he was, wouldn't her parents have tried to encourage her to choose him on her own? They hadn't. In fact, everything had been done in secrecy. Her parents saw her as a means to an end. And what happened if the man she was to marry did die? Legally, she'd be free to remarry whomever she wanted. But if her parents pressured her, again...

Rosalee drew in a shuddering breath. "I don't agree with what my father did to you," she said. "I'm sorry for it."

"It wasn't your fault," Aaron said, looking off in the distance. "So, you shouldn't apologize."

"No, but I feel the need to," she said quietly. "Now I understand why you were so upset when I offered you money."

He looked at her then. "I'm sorry too. I've been really unkind to you. You never gave me any reason to be. I guess I just...lumped you in with your father."

"It's understandable," she sighed. "But I accept your apology." She was quiet a moment. "I am at a loss as to what to do," she admitted. "The entire situation. It is as you said. Only one of us gets to walk away, with any measure of happiness."

He leaned back, slightly slumped against the bench. "Yep."

Rosalee looked around the small town, at least, what she could see from her seat. "You know, I almost feel as though I'm back home," she said.

"In that you feel happy here?" Aaron asked.

She shook her head. "No. I never truly felt at home. Not since we moved West. I enjoyed it back East. And Mother and I tried very hard to bring the things we enjoyed, such as social activities, out here. But after a time, it felt hollow. For the last while, I've been thinking about how lonely I feel. Even in the middle of a large crowd or party. I feel that here too. That's what I meant."

"I understand," Aaron said. "Like you just can't be yourself. Because of what others might think."

"Yes," she agreed, turning slightly to face him. "That's it, exactly!"

He gave a dry laugh, and angled himself toward her as well. "I don't believe it."

"Don't believe what?" she asked, with a small frown.

"That I'd have something in common with one of the wealthiest people around," he teased.

She laughed, but then a solemn feeling came over her. "I'm not sure if that's true anymore," she said.

"What do you mean?" he asked.

"Mother, when she let it slip that I was getting married, mentioned that Father needed this, that our finances were diminished."

Aaron's face grew troubled. "If that's the case," he said slowly, "you'd better watch yourself."

"How so?" Rosalee asked, tension filling her shoulders.

"Because your father isn't going to just let you go. Even if I did. Desperate men will go to any lengths they deem necessary."

His words chilled her, even though it was warm out. Almost hot. But he was right, she knew.

"Rosalee," he added, his eyes filled with something she couldn't describe, even if asked under oath, "I'm sorry. I'm being selfish, I know, wanting you to get on that train. But I..."

He didn't finish, and Rosalee didn't know what came over her, but she reached her hand toward his, resting it just a hair's breadth from his. Slowly, his fingers moved toward hers, and their hands brushed against each other.

"Don't say it. I know," she whispered. "But right now, can we just sit here? Pretend, just for a few moments, that none of this is happening?"

He nodded silently, and Rosalee felt a tear escape. Then another.

They sat there for at least a half hour, fingers barely touching, silent, just sitting. Strangely, for the first time that she could remember, Rosalee felt comfortable in the silence. She also didn't feel lonely. Even though they'd had a very rocky start to getting to know each other, and they still didn't really know each other that well, Rosalee felt they understood each other, and that meant a lot to her.

It was good to just sit. Though, despite what she'd asked, Rosalee's mind couldn't still. Her thoughts whirled, desperately trying to find a solution to her problem and Aaron's.

Should she give up her chance for freedom to clear him of an unfair debt? Was she unselfish enough to do that? Rosalee wasn't sure, and she knew Aaron felt the same. They were in an endless loop. The kind of situation where no matter what, no one would have a happy ending.

Now that she knew how he'd suffered at the hands of her father, Rosalee was sure even if she managed to escape the unwanted marriage, she'd be wracked with guilt for the rest of her life, and Aaron's life would be spent in a wrongful imprisonment.

Chapter 12

Breakfast was as filling as usual. Mrs. Harper sure set a fine table. Aaron was nearly bursting from all the biscuits and gravy he'd eaten. It was so good, though, he couldn't help himself.

The house was quiet, with most everyone out or in their rooms. Mrs. Harper was bustling about in her kitchen with the woman who helped her cook. Aaron glanced toward the study, where Rosalee sat looking out the window.

She'd been there for nearly an hour. And, like it or not, it was time for him to talk to her. Try to convince her it wouldn't be so bad to get on the train and get married. Sure, she didn't want to. But what if she was making a big deal out of nothing? It could be.

He was going to push all his guilt down deep inside and try to get her to see reason. There was a practical purpose for that too. If her father did show up, it would be a lot easier to pretend they'd missed the stage than it would be to tell him she wasn't going. With the former, he would still get his freedom.

Time was growing short. If her father was just a few days behind her, it wouldn't be long before he realized she wasn't there. If he even went. What if he hadn't? What if he had been watching, waiting to see what Aaron was doing? A cold sweat broke out on his forehead. They'd be in real trouble then.

She wasn't more than an hour and a half away from her home. Not far at all. Anyone could have recognized her. Gotten word to him. What would her father do if he came? Aaron knew the man's type. He wouldn't be happy. But would he hurt his daughter? As much as Aaron hoped the answer would be no, he wasn't sure. What he had to say was for her protection. No matter what he really wanted to say.

He stepped toward the study. She looked at him, then back out the window. "It won't work," she told him.

"What won't?" Aaron asked, sitting in one of the chairs near the sofa where she sat.

"Convincing me to go. It won't." She glanced at him. "I'm sorry."

"And I'm sorry I've got to try and get you there," Aaron said. "You know, it might not be so bad."

"It will be." Her voice was flat.

"Well, what makes you think so? After all, you've never met the guy."

"I just know."

He sighed. "I've got permission to drag you on that train. Kicking and screaming, remember? Those were your father's words. No one would think twice if I told them you weren't right in the head or an ill-behaved wife."

There was silence, then she looked at him. Her eyes were cold. "Try it. See what happens."

Aaron ran his fingers through his hair. "Now look. I don't want to do that. But, I deserve to have my life back. That's the only way I can get it. What if you just get on the train and get up there? You can run away there. Get to your aunt's. Then leave on another train somewhere once your father comes and sees you've arrived. Doesn't matter to me because I'll have done my part."

He was pleading with her. He knew that. But he was desperate. This seemed like a good idea. He'd thought of it last night and admittedly, was a little proud of it.

She seemed to think about that for a long moment. "That's not a bad idea," she finally agreed.

"See? So, what do you say? Pack? I'll see your trunks make it on the stage."

"I'm still thinking," she answered, and turned her attention out the window again.

"Why are you being so difficult?" Aaron asked, frustrated.

"You wouldn't understand," she told him, her own frustration evident.

"Try me."

"I don't want to marry him."

"Then don't," Aaron said. "Get up there and run away. Or don't. Find some other guy. It can't be that bad to marry a rich guy. You'll be rich. Richer. Isn't that what makes a woman happy? Unlimited dresses and travel and whatever else she wants?"

Rosalee said something, but it was so quiet Aaron couldn't hear it. "What's that?" he asked, leaning a little closer.

"Love," she said louder. "I want to marry for love."

That wasn't what he'd expected her to say.

"Have you ever been in love?" Rosalee asked.

Aaron hesitated. How could he answer that? There had been a woman. One he'd admired, foolishly. One who he grew fonder of each day. But he sure couldn't tell her that. He wasn't fully sure that was love.

"You have," she said. "I see it in your face."

He shrugged. "It's one sided," he told her. "She doesn't feel anything for me."

"It's still more than I have ever had."

He was going to answer, but Mrs. Harper walked past. "Look at you two!" she said with a broad smile. "Don't you look so good together! Will there be perhaps wedding bells in the future?"

As Aaron started to sputter, Rosalee grew a thoughtful expression and stood. "Mrs. Harper," she said. "That's a wonderful idea. Why, I can't be forced into marriage if I'm already married." She walked over to the older woman. "Tell me again about the single men here in town."

As the two women walked away, Aaron felt panic fill his every pore. If Rosalee got married, it might save her, but it would be the end of him. He couldn't let that happen.

Aaron jumped up, scrambling to follow, but not trying to appear as though he was listening, as he caught the tail end of their conversation.

"Quite well off! He owns four horses and a two-bedroom house," Mrs. Harper was saying. "His mother does live with them, though, and I understand she's quite demanding."

"I see. And the other?" Rosalee asked.

"Well, he's a good and hard-working man, though I'm not sure he'd be up to your standards," Mrs. Harper admitted. "He...well, he doesn't bathe too often, but perhaps that's just because he's not met a woman worth bathing for? He also has eight dogs. I think he's breeding them."

"Delightful," Aaron said, crossing his arms and leaning against the wall. "Both sound like real winners."

Rosalee and the boarding house owner turned to him. "What?" Aaron asked, widening his eyes in innocence. "I didn't realize this was a private conversation."

"It's not," Rosalee sniffed. "But if I have to make a sacrifice, then I want to know my options."

"They don't sound too great," Aaron said. "There's the alternative, you know. Go East."

"I told you," Rosalee said, crossing her arms over her chest as well, "that's not happening!"

"There is one more suggestion," Mrs. Harper said with a wide smile.

Aaron and Rosalee both looked at her. The boarding house owner winked, as she pushed open the kitchen door. "Marry each other!"

Rosalee's jaw dropped, and Aaron was pretty sure his did too. Before he'd unfrozen himself enough to think straight, Rosalee had gone up the stairs in a huff, and he went back to his post in his room, sitting, watching through the crack of the door, and trying to ignore the idea Mrs. Harper had planted.

Marry Rosalee... What would that be like?

Chapter 13

"Rosalee, would you do me a favor?" Mrs. Harper called.

"I'll be right there," Rosalee said, leaving the study and walking into the kitchen. When she entered, she wasn't expecting to see Mrs. Harper looking as though she were covered in snow. Most every inch of the woman was coated in a powdery white.

"What happened?" Rosalee gasped.

"A wind gust, just as I tripped holding the last of my flour," the boarding house owner said grimly. "Would you be willing to hurry to the general store and bring me back three pounds? Just tell Sam to put it on my account."

"Of course," Rosalee said. Mrs. Harper nodded at the kitchen door, and Rosalee scurried out. The general store wasn't far, just a few buildings down. She'd never gotten anything for Mrs. Harper before, and hoped that the shop owner would believe her and put the flour on her account.

As she reached the general store, Rosalee walked inside and stopped just a few paces within. She looked from side to side. Where was the flour? How did she get it? Cook had always done the shopping, and she wasn't quite sure what it would look like. Other than a white powder.

"Help you, miss?" a balding man asked from behind the counter.

Rosalee approached him in relief. "Yes, please. I'm one of Mrs. Harper's boarders. She asked me to fetch her three pounds of flour, on her account, as she's run out."

"I'll have it for you in just a moment," the man, she supposed might be Sam, said and reached under the counter to pull out a paper bag.

Rosalee took the opportunity to browse the store, gravitating over to the scented soaps. After sniffing several of them, she decided to come back tomorrow and purchase one.

Her fingers trailed along the books on a shelf, lace piled on a counter, and then her eyes fell on several hats. She was about to walk toward them when Sam called to her.

"Here you are, three pounds."

"Thank you," Rosalee said, hurrying over and accepting the bag.

With one last look around the store, she pushed open the store's door and stepped outside. A prickling struck the back of her neck, and Rosalee glanced around. She didn't see anyone. Was Aaron there? But why would he follow her? They were past that, surely.

She walked toward the boarding house, and had almost made it there, when the sudden urge to run struck her. Wrapping her arms around the bag of flour, she held it to her chest and started to speed up.

She'd almost made it to the house's back door when two arms grabbed her from behind. Rosalee screamed, and lunged forward, bending at the waist and twisting, attempting to get away.

Whoever grabbed her was much stronger than her, and they pulled her backward. Rosalee managed to scream again, just before a hand went over her mouth.

Panic filled her, and Rosalee wondered what was going to happen to her, just as the boarding house kitchen door opened, and an angry Mrs. Harper came running out, brandishing a rolling pin.

Rosalee clamped her teeth as hard as she could on the hand that had loosened. "Let me go!" she grunted, twisting again and trying to free herself.

The man holding her didn't seem to notice, and indeed, she hardly budged. She felt herself being dragged away.

A moment later, a blur rushed past her, tackling the man, forcing him away. He lost his balance, releasing Rosalee, and she managed to break away.

Frantically, she looked around for something to defend herself with. There was nothing. She was about fifty feet from the boarding house. Mrs. Harper was coming toward her as fast as she could, and Rosalee tried to move closer but tripped. She fell, and as she came to her knees saw Aaron.

He had been the blur! He had been the one to knock the man off of her. Aaron and her assailant were wrestling on the ground. Aaron was smaller, but was quick.

"Run," he grunted to Rosalee. "Hurry."

She hesitated, but when she saw the man reach for a knife, Rosalee reached in her specially sewn-in pocket and pulled out her Derringer, shooting the man in the arm.

The sound, though not very loud, still shook her, but Rosalee stayed still, pointing her weapon at the man, who was now groaning and had stopped fighting.

A small crowd had formed, and two men hauled her attacker away, with Mrs. Harper following them, shouting about how the man had attacked her boarder. Rosalee stood, watching, and then returned the Derringer to its hiding place, her hands trembling now that it was safe to.

Aaron approached her slowly. "You okay?" he asked.

"I might not have been," she said, stumbling toward him. "Not if you hadn't come." Her chest was rising and falling, and her entire body started to shake. "I don't know what's wrong with me," she gasped. "I can't stop. My throat feels tight, and I'm so cold."

"Shhh, I've got you," Aaron said, wrapping his arms around her. Rosalee laid her head on his chest. "Everything's all right. Just nerves, that's all. You just went through something scary. But everything's okay now. I'm here. You're safe."

His voice was gentle, soothing. She clung to him for several long moments, not wanting him to let her go, before she realized that they were in public. Hastily, she stepped back. "I-I'm sorry," she stammered.

"Don't be," he murmured, his eyes and voice gentle. "Not for that."

Their eyes locked, and Rosalee felt something wash over her that she didn't understand. Calm. A sense of rightness. She longed to be back in his arms. Her breathing was still rapid, only now it wasn't because she was frightened.

"You're a good shot," he told her with a grin, breaking the spell. "Where'd you learn to do that?"

"Before we moved out West, my mother was terrified we'd be attacked. She insisted Father teach us both to shoot. I didn't always carry mine with me back home, but it has been within reach since I came here, and I'm glad it was."

"I am too," Aaron told her. "You saved me a lot of bruising."

"You saved me from far more than that," Rosalee said. She shuddered. Then, worry filled her. "Do you think Father sent him?"

Mrs. Harper walked up just in time to overhear her. "No, dear. That man is a drunk. I'm ashamed to say we have a few around here. He told the sheriff he wanted to take a wife, and had decided on you."

Rosalee pressed her lips together. "That seems to be the story of my life." Then, she reached for Mrs. Harper's hand. "Thank you for coming when you did. Had you not..." She shook her head.

"I'm glad I distracted him enough for Mr. Woods to get him," the woman said. Then she laughed. "My dear! You are still holding the flour!"

Rosalee looked down, and then joined in the laughter. She was! And, despite all that had happened, the paper bag hadn't ripped open. "Here you are," she said, offering it. "As requested."

"A dedicated delivery girl," the woman said. "Now, let's get you inside. Some tea, and some rest."

Rosalee dutifully followed, Aaron right behind her. As they were walking inside, his hand rested on her lower back for a second, and a tingle filled her. Rosalee closed her eyes for just a moment. She could see herself spending more time with him. Indeed, her heart was telling her that she wanted to know Aaron better.

It was going to make what she had to do all the harder.

Chapter 14

Aaron followed the women into the boarding house. He almost wished he were a drinking man. He needed something to calm his nerves. When he'd seen Rosalee being dragged away, it had been all he could do not to beat the other man senseless. Truthfully, he might have, had Rosalee not shot him.

The fact she had still amazed him. He'd have never thought the woman could do that, let alone would. It made him admire her even more.

Aaron drew in a deep breath. He had to stop thinking about that. He knew what he had to do. It wasn't going to be easy, but Rosalee was worth it.

He rubbed at his eyes. He was exhausted. Sleep hadn't visited him since they'd arrived in Cottonwood Falls. First, there'd been the worry about getting her East. Then, worry about her marrying someone else. Each time he closed his eyes, her sweet face, her soft lips, her whispered voice filled his mind, making him unable to feel anything but torn and in pain.

Mrs. Harper poured them tea, then left the kitchen, realizing she'd run out of something else she needed for dinner, and wanted to get it herself.

Now alone, Aaron glanced at Rosalee. Her eyes were downcast, staring into her tea. He saw something floating in it, a bit of tea leaf likely, and wondered if that's what she was watching, letting her eyes follow its path.

Unless she was in shock.

"You okay?" Aaron asked.

"I'm angry at myself," Rosalee said.

He wasn't expecting that. Too surprised to answer for a moment, he finally said, "Why?"

"Because I got myself into this whole mess."

"That's not entirely true," he told her. "Your father has a part in this."

"Be that as it may," Rosalee said, "I've realized something. All my life I've been spoiled. Acted selfish." She set her tea down. "By getting off of the stagecoach, without any plan in mind, I acted rashly. Perhaps I thought things would just work out for me, as they always had. I'm furious at my actions. I've messed things up horribly for myself."

Aaron didn't know what to say. She wasn't wrong, she had made some mistakes, but he didn't like how she was blaming herself for reacting to a situation she'd been thrown into. Sometimes, when a person was put into something unexpectedly, they reacted in a way that they might not have, if they'd had time to rationally think things through. He couldn't fault her for that. He'd likely had a few of those knee-jerk instances himself. Everyone had, at one point or another.

He wished he knew what to say to make her feel better. Was there something? He didn't really have experience in this sort of thing.

Rosalee interrupted his thoughts. "There's no need for you to look so…" she waved her hand around, "whatever it is that you are feeling. This is my problem, not yours."

"Have you forgotten that what affects you also affects me? That our fates are sort of entwined?"

"No, I haven't," she answered stiffly. "And I know what I'm going to do."

"So, you'll get on the train?" Aaron asked. "Or are you looking to get a husband? Because if it's the second—"

"It's none of your business," she said, raising her chin.

"It's completely my business!" Aaron argued. He gestured between them. "Remember? Us? Two different goals, but same problem. You don't want to go, and I've got to get you there."

"You don't have to remind me," Rosalee snapped. "I'm well aware of the situation."

"I'm not trying to make you mad," Aaron said. "I just don't understand. What's the big deal? You're talking about marrying someone here, because if you're married, then you can't be married to the person your father has planned. What's the difference? Both of them are strangers. You don't know what you'd be getting into with either. But at least with the guy your father chose, you'd be well off."

"Money isn't everything," Rosalee said, and crossed her arms.

"Spoken like someone who's had it her whole life," he retorted. "But when you're cold or hungry or don't have a roof over your head...you start missing it real quick."

"Fine. I won't get married," Rosalee sniffed. "I didn't like my options around here anyway."

"What will you do then?" Aaron asked, trying his best not to grit his teeth. She was so frustrating. Were all women this way?

"Run." Her eyes widened then. "You could do that too. We could both run away. Together, separate. It doesn't matter. Leave. Start fresh."

Aaron could tell the idea excited her, but he shook his head slowly. "It's not a good idea."

"Why not?" she asked.

"Because if you run, you'll spend the rest of your life looking over your shoulder. That's no way to live. Always worried you'll be caught. That someone will find you or learn your secret. It's no good. Besides, how would you manage on your own? What can you do to earn your living?"

She sighed heavily, and pushed her tea toward the middle of the table and dropped her head into her hands. "You're right. I hate it, but you're right."

"We both know how this will end," he said.

"There's got to be another way out of this mess for both of us," she said, looking up at him with determination. "We just have to find it."

He shook his head, not believing a word she said. It was impossible. Only one of them was going to have anything remotely like a happy ending. Not for the first time, Aaron wished he'd never gone to look at the horse that day. He closed his eyes, and sent a prayer to the heavens that if there was a way they could both walk away from this situation, they would.

A soft touch on his hand startled him, and his eyes flew open. Rosalee was looking at him with a sad smile. Aaron reacted without thinking, and captured her hand in his, laying a kiss in her palm.

Chapter 15

Rosalee let out a soft gasp, as Aaron's lips pressed into her palm. Her eyes met his, and her heart started to pound, as he slowly released her hand.

"I shouldn't have done that," he said, eyes still locked on hers. "I'm not sure why I did."

She couldn't answer. Her mouth was dry and her chest too tight to properly draw in a breath. He still hadn't looked away. Why had he done that? It solidified her decision. She had to do it now.

As though it was the last time she was going to see him, Rosalee tried to fix Aaron in her mind. His broad shoulders, his hair that didn't quite want to behave. Eyes, so expressive.

She was going to make the right decision. Not for her father or mother. Not even for herself. But, she was going to try to right a wrong. She might not be able to restore the time that Aaron had lost, but she could see no more of it was wasted. Even at the cost she loathed. That was the one thing she could do for him. It would make the rest of her life at least a measure easier.

"Rosalee," Aaron said softly, his eyes filled with worry. "Why are you crying?"

Blinking a few times, she put a hand to her cheek, surprised to find it wet from tears. When had those fallen? "I don't know. Maybe because," she told him sadly, "I know what I have to do."

The tiny muscles in his face tightened. "Do I want to know?" he asked.

She gave a small laugh and shrugged. "Oh, Aaron. It's all so complicated." Rosalee rose from her chair and paced around the kitchen. She paused and turned to him. "I've put you into a terrible spot. I have. Worse, the longer I'm around you, the more I feel guilty about what my father did, and I want to fix it somehow."

"You don't need to fix anything." He stood by his chair, watching her. "It's not your place."

Rosalee crossed to him in two long steps and put her finger to his lips. "Don't. Please. Let me finish. This is hard enough." Her voice caught as she continued, "When the next stage comes, I'll get on it. The train too. I'll go East. Marry that man. You've been through enough. Too much. Unjustly. And I won't be the cause of more of that. I couldn't live with myself if I were."

The shock on his face was almost enough to make her feel better, and surely it was something she'd remember for years to come, but Rosalee continued in a rush, her words filled with every bit of the pain and heartache swelling in her. "You, though. You need to go after the woman you are in love with. If you don't, you'll live with regrets. I know you've lost time. There's no fixing that. But maybe she's still there, waiting for you. Maybe it's not too late for that."

Rosalee dropped her hand, and stood, facing him, closer than was likely proper. Her words had dried up, which was good because she knew if she said any more, they'd tremble, and she didn't want to appear weak.

To her surprise, Aaron reached up and let his fingers trace her cheek. His touch was thrilling, yet left a strange hollow inside of her when he removed his hand. "Rosalee," he whispered. "I can't go after her."

"Why not?" she asked, her eyes searching his face. "One of us should be happy."

He drew in a shuddering breath. "Because that woman, the one I'm in love with? Who I fell in love with from afar? She's you."

Chapter 16

Aaron could tell by the stunned expression on Rosalee's face that wasn't what she'd expected. Before he got sick from the nerves filling his stomach, he forced himself to keep talking.

"I don't know that you going there is the right thing. Especially not because of me," he told her. "I don't want you to marry him. I want you to marry me. But I can't ask you for that. You don't know me. I'm practically a stranger. A fool who fell in love with a woman who doesn't know him. It's no better than you marrying that man."

He wanted to say more. Knew he ought to. The more he said, the more he could ramble. Buy time before his heartache spilled out through his words, before the pain he'd been feeling each time he thought about her as a married woman came to life.

Her mouth was moving, opening and closing. Finally, she gasped out, "Me? But, you don't know me."

"You're right," he told her, then ran his fingers through his hair. "Which is why it's stupid. The whole thing is. I don't know how it happened. Just, I saw you sometimes. And your face stayed in my mind. As much as I tried to hate you because of who you were, because of your father, I couldn't." Desperation filled his voice. "Now, knowing you better...you are all I think about. How I want to help you. How I care for you. How I can't let you go and marry him. I can't. Especially if it's for my sake."

"But it's the only way," Rosalee cried, "don't you see? You are here because of me. If I leave, then you get your life back."

"Oh, Rosalee," Aaron sighed, daring to touch her soft cheek again before dropping his hand. "I'll be okay. Somehow. You go. Find something and someone who makes you happy. Talk to your parents. Maybe they've got someone else they can choose that would make them and you happy."

"But what of you?" she asked, her lip quivering.

He shook his head. "I'll run."

"But you said running was a bad idea," Rosalee said.

"Well...it's not a good idea, but I can't work for your father forever," Aaron told her. He closed his eyes a moment, then as he opened them admitted, "The only thing keeping me there wasn't risk of my neck."

"What was it then?" she asked.

"The glimpses of you," he whispered. "And the fool hope you'd glance my way."

She was quiet for so long that Aaron felt his heart shatter. Why had he confessed such a thing? Put even more weight and worry on her? He'd opened his mouth to apologize, when she spoke.

"I did see you."

He stilled. "You did?"

"Yes. I...I asked about you. Your name. Sometimes, I'd go walking around the house, hoping to see you. Maybe say hello." She wet her lips nervously. "But, I have a secret," she said softly.

"Is it something I should know? About the situation?" Aaron asked, slightly worried.

Her cheeks pinked, and she blushed. "Not really. It's just...I didn't recognize you on the stage because I'd never really seen you so close. You see, without my...without my spectacles, I can't see great distances."

"Is that all?" Aaron stared at her incredulously. "With everything that's been going on, you're concerned what I'd think about you not seeing so well far off?"

"My mother," she began, and then she stopped.

"Ah. She told you they weren't becoming?" At her small nod, Aaron scowled. "Sounds like something she'd do. It also makes sense, then, why you didn't recognize me. Here I thought you'd always just been haughty." He raised her chin gently in his hand, and said, "You wear them when you need to. It doesn't bother me a bit. I bet you look adorable in them."

Her cheeks reddened further. Then, something came to mind, and he stiffened.

"What is it?" Rosalee gasped, glancing around as though for danger.

"I'm just thinking when I say my prayers tonight, I'm going to be real thankful that when you shot your Derringer, you didn't miss and hit me because you couldn't see."

"Oh you," she laughed, and smacked at his shoulder. "I could see just fine. It's far away I can't see well."

"Still," he said, seriously, pointing upward. "Thanks are in order."

Before either of them could say anything else, Mrs. Harper walked in with a strange look on her face. "I'm glad you are both here," she said, glancing between them.

"What's wrong?" Rosalee asked. "Is it about that man who attacked me? Do I need to speak to the sheriff?"

The older woman hesitated, then shook her head. "No, dear, I'm afraid it might be worse."

All of the color drained out of Rosalee's face, and she staggered over to the small table and sat heavily in one of the chairs. "Oh no," she whispered, dropping her head in her hands.

"What?" Aaron asked, wondering what he'd missed.

Mrs. Harper took a deep breath, and moved to Rosalee, putting her hand on her shoulder. "There's a man in town. He's asking everyone about Rosalee. Says she's his daughter and she may be here against her will."

Aaron's head snapped toward the window, and using the curtain for as much cover as he could, glanced out into the street. He didn't see anyone he recognized passing by. Leaning closer to the glass, he angled himself to see as far as he could up one side of the road and down the other.

"Does he know I'm here?" he could hear Rosalee ask behind him.

"Yes, I think so," Mrs. Harper said. "The man who runs the stage office pointed him to the boarding house."

"This is it," Rosalee said. "There's no running." Her voice was calm. Frightfully so.

"We'll tell him we missed the stage," Aaron said. "That you intended to get on the next one." But even as the words passed his lips, he didn't feel as confident as he hoped he sounded.

She didn't have time to answer, before there was a loud knocking on the front door of the boarding house. The door opened, and heavy footsteps sounded outside the kitchen door. Mrs. Harper's face was worried. "I don't want trouble," she said quietly.

"And you won't have it," Rosalee promised, even though her face was filled with dread. She plastered on a smile Aaron knew was meant to be reassuring for the other woman, though she likely felt anything but. She stood from the chair. "He's my father. I'll go."

Beyond the door, they could hear her father calling out, "Rosalee. Show yourself. I know you're here."

His voice boomed through the boarding house, and the anger in it was barely contained.

Aaron grabbed her hand. Rosalee squeezed it gently, then whispered, "We might not have had much time together, but I do know one thing."

"What's that?" he asked.

"I think I could love you."

And before he could even take his next breath, Rosalee had pushed through the kitchen door.

Chapter 17

"There's no need to shout. I'm right here," Rosalee said quietly. She stepped into the foyer and indicated the sitting room. "Would you like to sit?"

"No. I'd like to know why my daughter is here, instead of back East, like she was told to be," her father said. Then, before she could answer, he added, "It wasn't an accident either, or your trunks would have arrived without you."

Rosalee pressed her lips together. "You're right."

"Then what have you to say for yourself?" her father growled. "Your mother is frantic. I'm angry. How could you scare us like this? It's a good thing one of the hands came here for supplies and saw you. If it hadn't been for him getting me word, I'd have been on that train myself, none the wiser. Was that what you wanted?"

"I wanted time to think," Rosalee said, studying her father. She wasn't sure how much she should admit that she knew, but thought to herself at this point, it didn't really matter if she explained she knew she was to marry. Nothing she said could make the situation worse.

"Time to think? Time to *think*?" Her father's voice rose on the echo.

"That's right." Rosalee tilted her head slightly. "After all, if I'm going to be married, there's a lot to think about."

Her father's jaw hung for a moment. "I see. And just what is it you have to ponder?"

"The unfairness of it all," Rosalee answered frankly. "I wasn't consulted."

"You don't have to be," her father said. "And I would think you are aware of that. You're a woman and my daughter. Your life is mine to do with as I please."

"Even if that means you force me to go, kicking and screaming?" Rosalee watched his eyes narrow, but he didn't seem to pick up on her insinuation.

"If that's what it takes," he answered.

"I thought there would be some consideration afforded to me, even if it was simply telling me in advance, not hiding that you were ridding yourself of me to take control of a company."

"I'm not ridding myself of you. It's a necessary thing," her father said. "A shrewd business deal. But I have it on good authority that he's ill. You might be a widow in a year. Maybe sooner. Accidents happen all the time."

The words almost seemed to hold a threat. Or a promise. But who would the accident happen to? Would her father really do such a thing? Days before, Rosalee would never have thought so. Now, she wasn't so sure of anything other than the fact that her father was nothing like the man she'd known him to be.

He was ruthless. Greedy. Conniving.

"And until then?" Rosalee asked. She shook her head. "That's not all I know about."

Just then, Aaron came through the kitchen door. Her father's face turned a deep shade of red, he was so angry. "You!" he roared. "It would have been better off for you if you were dead. You were supposed to see my daughter safely to her aunt."

"I was trying to," Aaron said. "I didn't expect her to trick me—more than once, mind you. She's a far sight smarter than most may give her credit for."

Though his words warmed her, even in that fearful moment, Rosalee's father sneered, and she felt her stomach clench.

"You had a job to do," he said, his voice full of anger. "Forget about trying to repay the debt. You'll be hanging before sundown. You're just as worthless as you are irritating."

Rosalee gasped. "Why would you do that? What did he ever do to you?"

"The boy's not good," her father said, not even looking her way. "You wouldn't understand."

"I understand everything," Rosalee said, straightening to her full height. "Including how you've taken away all he holds dear. His freedom."

"It's just business," her father said, shrugging. "If he even told you the truth. His kind doesn't."

"Dirty business," Rosalee retorted. "And you seem to know all about that."

"It's nothing you need to worry about," her father said. "Now, I'm staying at the hotel. You'll pack, immediately, and stay in my suite until the stage comes. I'm taking you East. You won't be out of my sight until the ring is on your finger."

"I'm not going," Rosalee said firmly.

"You will," her father answered.

"Let me finish. Perhaps you'll even like what I say." She crossed her arms. "I'm not going until you promise to release Mr. Woods from his wrongful debt. Right here, right now. In writing. Cleared, and you'll never bother him again."

"Don't," Aaron said, stepping up to Rosalee and putting a hand on her arm. "I'm not worth it, Rosalee."

"You got that right. Take your filthy hands off my daughter," her father snarled. "How dare you call her by her first name."

Aaron held his hands up, and took a half step closer to her father, putting himself at an angle between them. "There's no need to get angry. You might not believe it, but I have been looking after her."

"Is that so?" her father sneered. "Or have you been looking *at* her?"

Rosalee stiffened. "He saved my life, Father. From a man who was intent on taking me for his own. He deserves to be released from your unfair debt, if for no other reason."

"He deserves to—"

"Also know the real reason you ruined my life," Aaron said, stepping closer. "If I'm going to hang, I at least deserve that."

"Aaron," Rosalee whispered.

He shook his head at her. "I want to know," he said.

Her father's face grew considering, and he nodded. "Very well. It doesn't matter. Why not? I'd heard about you. Your talent for picking horses. You were just starting out, but had the makings of a good breeder. A friend of mine was trying to do the same. You were in the way. It was as simple as that. I got you out of the way; he got me something I wanted later."

Rosalee stared at him in shock, while Aaron bitterly said, "So, it wasn't personal? You were just looking after a friend. Getting a future favor. I bet you didn't even want that horse, did you?"

"That's right." Her father crossed his arms. "Happy now? It was just business. Always is, boy."

"I cannot believe you'd do such a thing," Rosalee said. She shook her head. "Where is my father? The kind man? The one who, I thought, cared for me. Was a good, honest man."

Her father laughed then, and the sound was cold and bitter. "Kind and good and honest don't make money, Rosalee. Don't put dresses on your back, jewels around your neck, a fancy house and parties at your fingertips. If you want the nicer things in life, you've got to make sacrifices. And you and your mother? You always want the nice things."

It was true. She had always wanted them. However, now...

"If I'd known that the clothes I wore came at such a cost," Rosalee said softly, "I'd as soon have walked around naked."

As both men stared at her in shock, Rosalee refused to blush. If her cheeks were pink—or red—it was from anger, nothing more, she told herself.

"If your mother could hear you," her father began.

"I think she'd be disappointed in me," Rosalee agreed. "But no more so than I am in myself, for going all these years without learning what kind of man my father really was, and how he got his fortune. It's becoming clear to me that Mother was aware as well, and had no quarrel about such terrible acts. I'm ashamed of the name Milton."

"We all make sacrifices," her father repeated. He pointed toward the stairs. "It's time for you to make yours. Enough of this foolish, futile game. Go pack."

"Rosalee." Aaron's voice was tight. Urgent. He was trying to tell her something.

Nearly frozen to the spot, she shook her head at her father, ignoring Aaron. Whatever it was couldn't be nearly as important as what was pressing on her heart. "No. Father, release his debt."

"Rosalee," Aaron said again. She felt his eyes blazing into her. When he said her name again, she reluctantly turned toward him.

"Run," he told her, with a jerk of his head toward the door.

"Where?" she whispered.

Her father stepped closer, but Aaron pushed her away, blocking her father's attempt to grab her. Rosalee stumbled, and her back hit the wall near the kitchen door. As her father lunged at her, Aaron blocked him again.

"It doesn't matter where. I'll hold him off as long as I can. If I'm not hanged, I'll be in jail. But it's worth it. All of it. The rest of my days—or minutes—no matter how few, I'll be content knowing you got away. This is all I can do for you. To show you how much I love you."

At his words, everything stopped. Her father stared between them in a mixture of anger and fear. Aaron's expression was one of determination, and Rosalee felt goosebumps break out over her entire body.

A choking sob ripped from Rosalee's throat. Her chest felt as though it were being torn apart. She couldn't bear to see the desperation on Aaron's face, and the anger on her father's. How had everything changed so quickly?

Rosalee reached toward Aaron, and her fingers brushed against his arm. Then, she burst through the kitchen door and ran.

Chapter 18

"How dare you, boy." Rosalee's father growled, and pushed him, but Aaron refused to let him through the kitchen door Rosalee had run through. "Love? You filthy no-good. You should know your place."

"I do," Aaron said, ducking as her father swung at him. "It's right here. Seeing that Rosalee gets away from the likes of you. Doesn't matter to me if she loves me back or not. I'm doing this to help her."

"To help her? You don't know anything, do you?" Mr. Milton stepped back, his hands at his sides. "You wouldn't, though. You don't have a wife. A daughter. A business. Sometimes you have to do things you don't want to do. But you'll never understand that. Not a nothing like you."

"I could have," Aaron said, his own fists still raised, "but you took any chance of that away from me the minute you lied about me trying to steal that horse."

"You just can't let the past go, can you? And because of that, you've ruined my daughter."

"I've not ruined her. I'd never hurt her, not in any way. But you don't understand that people aren't your chess pieces to just move around as you want, for your personal gain." Aaron stood firm, still against the door, hoping that Rosalee had gotten away. Perhaps Mrs. Harper had helped her. He didn't know where they'd go, but he hoped it was for help.

Mr. Milton paced a few steps one way, then the next. Before Aaron realized it, he'd run out the front door and into the street.

"Get the sheriff! This man kidnapped and violated my daughter!" Mr. Milton yelled loudly. "Help! Help me!"

Aaron's jaw dropped. He staggered outside in disbelief. As much as he wanted to run himself, look for Rosalee, he knew if he let her father out of his sight, things could be much worse. And then the accusation he'd violated Rosalee?

Before he knew what was happening, a crowd had formed, staring at them. Someone stood next to him, and he glanced over to see who it was. Mrs. Harper looked angry, her rolling pin in one hand as she shook it.

"He has not harmed anyone," she said loudly. "This man," she pointed at Rosalee's father, "is forcing his daughter into an unwanted marriage."

The crowd's eyes switched from staring at him, to staring at Mr. Milton.

Mr. Milton stepped forward, shaking his head. "So, you know she's supposed to get married? What's your part in all of this, woman? Is this a house of sin? Have you played a role in keeping my daughter here? Are there other young women here against their will?"

There was an audible gasp from the crowd that was growing, and all eyes swung toward Mrs. Harper, who was sputtering.

"Leave her out of this," Aaron said. "The marriage decision is between you and your daughter. The debt, which you've admitted is false, is between you and me. So, when the sheriff gets here, I think he should hear all of us speak. Perhaps he can act as a neutral party with some advice on how best to handle this situation."

"And buy my willful daughter time to get away?" Rosalee's father turned side to side, seeking her.

"What you're doing is wrong," Aaron warned, stepping closer, drawing the man's attention again. He wasn't sure how long he could keep it, but he hoped to buy Rosalee every minute he could. He also hoped someone had called for the sheriff.

"You can't use people the way you do. I know she's not the only one you've done that to. Nor am I the only one. I know several of your other men were threatened into silence for the things you do with your business. Others, they don't care since they get a piece of it."

Mr. Milton's face turned a deep crimson. "You talk of things you know nothing about," he said, raising a finger in warning. "When the sheriff gets here, he'll hear the truth."

"What truth?" Aaron snorted. "You've already admitted—"

"I've admitted nothing," her father roared, stepping closer to him.

Aaron could tell he was getting angry. The crowd was watching closely. In the distance, Aaron could see several others headed their way. This might be his only chance to get a public confession from the man, and clear his name, because Mr. Milton was right. He'd admitted to nothing in front of others.

If Aaron didn't act quickly, he'd be hanging, thanks to Mr. Milton and his friend the judge on his side. Aaron had to get him to confess.

An idea came to mind, and Aaron lowered his head. He looked up, and said, "I just want my freedom. You know I didn't try and steal anything. Rosalee is your daughter. I understand that. You're responsible for her. You have every right to do with her what you will. But you and I...we aren't related. I was a stranger. One who stood between you and something you wanted. That's not a crime. It's an inconvenience. You buy so many people off. Why didn't you offer that to me?"

He took a deep breath. "Why couldn't you have just let me go? Bought the horse. Let me live my life? Even just warn me away. I'd have left. It was a horse. Sure, I wanted it. But I want my freedom more. I can get another horse. But I only get so many hours to live. Why did you have to take away all that I had?"

"I told you," Mr. Milton said with a shrug, and surprise in his voice. "I don't know what part you aren't understanding. It was business. Just like Rosalee's marriage is."

"But do you even know what you're sending her into?" Aaron asked. "Do you even know if he's a good man? If he'll treat her well?"

Mr. Milton's face flickered with uncertainty. "It's…"

"I know. It's business," Aaron said, shaking his head in disgust. "But I hope one day your eyes open and you see all of the lives that you've ruined from all of your business decisions. Now, I can't stop you from doing what you want with Rosalee, you're right. But I can put a stop to what you've been doing to me."

"And just how are you going to do that?" Mr. Milton sneered. "It's your word against mine."

"Not exactly," Aaron said. He nodded toward Mrs. Harper. "I hate to bring you into it, ma'am, but I'm sure you heard his confession earlier. You were in the kitchen with us when he arrived."

"I did," the older woman said, nodding.

"As did I," the other male boarder Aaron recognized from the dinner table said, stepping forward from the crowd. "I was about to walk into the house when I heard everything from the porch."

"I heard it from upstairs," a woman, another boarder, said, coming closer.

"And I've heard quite a few things," a man said, coming up behind Mr. Milton. "Sheriff Wilson, at your service."

"Thank goodness you're here, Sheriff," Mr. Milton said, turning at once. "Albus Milton. This man has coerced my daughter. Bent her to his will. Confused her. He even claims to love her. You know how easily a woman can be wooed with sweet words. It's dangerous. She has no experience with men. However, she's already promised to another. I'm fearful this man right here has not only ruined her reputation, but also her future. I demand he be arrested."

"That so?" the sheriff asked, crossing his arms and staring Aaron up and down.

"Yes," Rosalee's father agreed. A smirk began to form on his face.

Aaron started to feel worried. Here were both boarders, along with Mrs. Harper, who had said they overheard her father. How could the sheriff be taking the man's side? The man's sway upset him. How many were in his pocket?

"We need to find my daughter," Mr. Milton said. He waved his arms about. "Can't anyone do anything right in this backwards town? What's taking so long? Arrest him. Make him say where he told her to hide."

"I'm not hiding, Father," Rosalee's voice said, as she pushed through the crowd.

Aaron watched as she drew closer. Her eyes were sorrowful as she looked at him. "I'm sorry, Father," she said. "But I've told the sheriff everything I know. It might not be a lot, but it's enough to—"

Her father stiffened. "You lied, you mean."

"It sure didn't sound like a lie," Sheriff Wilson said. He made a motion, and two men stepped forward, each taking one of Mr. Milton's arms. "Matter of fact, she had quite a bit to say. Like how you've been keeping Mr. Woods against his will, under false pretenses and threats. Luckily for us, the circuit judge rides through here tomorrow. We're going to let him work this all out."

Before Aaron quite knew what was happening, Mr. Milton was being escorted away. The crowd slowly broke up, whispering among themselves. The boarders went inside, as did Mrs. Harper. Aaron found himself suddenly, and uncomfortably, all alone with Rosalee.

Chapter 19

Everything had been happening so quickly, and now it felt as though time had frozen. It should have shocked Rosalee that her father had been taken away. Horrified her, even. Yet...she felt a profound sense of relief.

That was very quickly followed by fear, as practicality sank in. Whatever wrongdoings her father was accused of or were discovered about him meant, without a doubt, that her life was going to change dramatically. As would her mother's. It was possible they would no longer be well off.

At the thought of her mother, Rosalee's heart sank even further. Her mother would be devastated. And angry. She was sure to blame Rosalee, and, in a way, she had been part of this. Had brought about her father's downfall, as it were. No matter it had been the right thing to tell the truth, to beg the sheriff to come and help Aaron.

The fact remained, she was responsible for her father's arrest.

Rosalee drew in a shuddering breath, and looked out across Cottonwood Falls. The town had very quickly gone back to its usual ways. People walking in twos or threes, a soft breeze carrying dust and warmth and the faint scent of horses from a distance.

She tried very hard to focus on those things around her, and not the terrible ache she was feeling in her chest. Her father had often talked about the betrayal of others. He'd likely never imagined his own daughter would do that to him. Nor had she.

Aaron let out a sigh, and she glanced his way. He had his hands in his pockets. "Now what?" he asked.

"I was wondering the same," she admitted.

"Well, we could go our separate ways," Aaron told her. "Though that doesn't quite seem like the right thing to do. I reckon there will be need for me to stay for a few days. Tell my side to the judge. I'm...I'm sorry, Rosalee. I never thought any of this would happen."

"Neither did I," she answered quietly. "But it has happened, and there's no going back. Only forward."

He nodded. "What do you think you'll do?"

"I think that all depends very much on what happens with the judge. If everything is taken away, I'll have to start fresh. Even if it's not, I plan to do the same. I won't take anything from my father at all. My grandparents left me a small inheritance. I can use that," she said. "I have complete control over it, next month on my birthday."

He toed his boot in the dust, and answered, "That's good."

"Aaron," she said, walking over to him, "I think you are feeling guilty. Please don't be."

"I've upended your life," he told her, his eyes meeting hers. "Of course I'm feeling some guilt."

"Father started it," she reminded him. "And, truthfully, you didn't do anything wrong. All of it was me. I'm the one who got off the stage. I'm the one who struck you with the stick. I'm the one who—"

"Went against her father to try and get my freedom, even at the cost of her own," he interrupted. "Why?"

"You were willing to hang or be imprisoned for me," she whispered. "Why?"

"Because...because..."

Aaron's face was one of hesitation. Of fear.

"What you said, earlier," Rosalee started, "that you loved me. Did you mean that? Or was that one of those things a person sometimes says in a moment, but isn't true?"

"I meant it," Aaron said, his face honest. "And when you said you could love me...did you mean that?"

"I did."

They were quiet for a long moment, neither of them moving. Finally, Aaron's fingers reached for hers, and Rosalee accepted his warm, rough hand around hers.

"I'm scared," she whispered, stepping closer, and resting her head against his chest. "Everything I thought I knew or had has been ripped away from me."

"Not everything," Aaron said, putting a hand on her back. "Not your strength or courage, not your wit or your ability to care for others."

"Yes, but my name." She looked up at him, tears in her eyes. "I used to be so proud to be a Milton. Now, the name weighs heavily upon me."

He was quiet, and Rosalee had thought he'd never answer, when he asked, "Well, what about Woods?"

"What about it?" she asked, confused.

"If you're ashamed of the name Milton, you could be a Woods. Mrs. Woods."

Her breath caught in her chest. "Is that...is that a proposal?"

He shrugged, and his cheeks turned a hint of red. "I know it's soon. And I know I'm maybe not who you wanted. But, if one day, if you keep on liking me..."

Rosalee laughed. For the first time in months, she felt light and happy, almost as if she had no worries at all, which was quite silly when she thought about it, considering the day she'd had.

"Is that a yes, maybe?" Aaron asked, scratching at his head.

"Oh yes, most assuredly, that's a yes," Rosalee told him.

"There's something you've got to know, though," Aaron said, stepping away from her and looking at her with such a serious expression, Rosalee's smile faltered.

"What is it?" she asked.

"You've got to know that I can't give you all the things you deserve or all of the things that you're used to," he said. "A huge fancy house, servants, dresses, travel. I'm not a wealthy man. But I can give you myself. All my love. The promise that I'm going to do my best to prove that I'm worthy of you."

"I'm not asking for anything else," Rosalee told him. "Even if I never get another new dress in my life, I'll be content with you by my side. You've had a dream ripped from you, and I want to be with you, to watch it realize. That's all I want."

Aaron's face neared hers, and just as he started to lean down, and his lips brushed against hers, Mrs. Harper called from the boarding house. "Mr. Woods! Miss Milton! Hurry inside!"

Chapter 20

Aaron and Rosalee burst into the house in a near panic. Rosalee was reaching toward her pocket, while Aaron's fists were at the ready.

"My goodness," the boarding house owner said. "Calm down!"

"Calm down? You sounded urgent!" Rosalee said. "What's happened?"

"Nothing, I hope," the woman said, with raised brows. "I was trying to help."

"Help with what?" Aaron asked.

There was a heavy sigh from Mrs. Harper. "To save the both of you from being more of a public spectacle than you already are. Why, this will be something the town talks about for weeks!"

"Ah. I suppose we should thank you then," Rosalee said.

Aaron nodded. "Yes. You keep coming to the rescue. Reckon I owe you more than a thanks."

"Just this week's rent," the woman said, and turned toward the kitchen. "And a wedding invitation."

Rosalee laughed softly, and nodded. Alone again, she turned to Aaron. "I need to go write Mother. Explain things. If she doesn't know already."

"Of course. I'm here if you need me. While I hope the excitement is over, don't...don't go outside without me. Just in case."

"I promise," Rosalee said.

He watched as she climbed the stairs, feeling a hint of sadness on her. Aaron had no doubt it would be difficult for her to write to her mother, and he just hoped that he'd be able to give her the support that she needed when she returned downstairs.

The rest of the evening was quiet. Dinner was subdued, and afterward, everyone read or sewed.

He'd then had a restless night, and couldn't imagine just how Rosalee felt. Her entire world had been turned upside down. Though this was a little different, he knew how he'd felt those first few days when all he'd known had changed. Yet, the next morning at breakfast, she'd looked as calm and composed as she always did.

Except for the slight quiver in her lips when Mrs. Harper asked how she was. He kept darting glances at her, half in awe that Rosalee had returned his affections, and the rest of him sure she'd change her mind.

After breakfast, the three of them walked to the schoolhouse that had been turned into a temporary courtroom. It seemed like most of the town was there, crowded around, standing at every window and near the door, since there wasn't room inside.

Aaron, Rosalee, and Mrs. Harper were permitted inside, along with the two boarders who were potentially going to be witnesses. Rosalee sat quietly next to Aaron, as they waited for the judge. The sheriff stood in front of the room, arms crossed, glancing around at everyone as they whispered quietly.

"I feel sick," Rosalee admitted quietly. "I know I'm doing the right thing, but it feels wrong."

"Of course it does. It's your father," Aaron said. "I don't blame you. No one does."

The judge walked in just then, and everyone stood. He faced the room and cleared his throat. "I'm here today for seven cases," he said, "Walter versus Jones, Smith and the theft of two goats..."

As the judge continued to say the cases he'd hear, Aaron glanced over at Rosalee. Her face was pale, and her hands were clasped together tightly. Silently, he rested one of his hands on hers.

"And in the case of Mr. Milton," the judge finished, "he has asked for his lawyers, and to return East as there is no concrete evidence of the wrongdoings he is accused of. It is the court's opinion that any complaints about his business practices will need to be brought forth by those who feel they experienced wrongdoings. Arrangements are being made for his departure as we speak."

Rosalee gasped, and Aaron felt anger surge from him. Beside him, he could feel Rosalee shaking, from fear or hurt or upset he wasn't sure, and put his arm around her shoulders.

Sheriff Wilson stepped forward. "The first case will begin in five minutes. All those who wish to leave may."

Rosalee stood hurriedly and went outside. Aaron followed close behind her. Neither spoke as they left the schoolyard, continued down the street, and found themselves alone.

Aaron wasn't sure what to say. Everything that kept coming to mind might very well be the wrong thing. After what had just happened, he didn't want to upset Rosalee any more than she already was.

With Mr. Milton going East, he was likely to either get a fancy lawyer to help him or vanish, never to be seen. It wouldn't be hard for a man like that to even still run his business, but under a silent partner's name, while he personally distanced himself.

Maybe it was far-fetched. Maybe it wasn't. Not for a man like that, one who had spent his whole life out for one thing. Success. Aaron had no idea what he'd do. But he sure hoped neither he nor Rosalee would be tangled up in it.

"I've been thinking," Rosalee said suddenly.

The sound of her voice startled Aaron. He'd been lost in thoughts and didn't realize just how far they'd walked.

Aaron glanced at Rosalee then. "What about?" he said.

"About how I want to put this behind me. I spent a long time thinking about this last night. I had the feeling Father would do something like this. I don't know what will happen, but for myself, I'd like to distance myself from whatever happens. In truth, he committed no crime toward me. He was within his rights to promise my hand in marriage. However, what he did to you..."

"I've got my freedom now," Aaron told her. "I don't plan to ask for any sort of restitution. In truth, I never want to see the man again. Which makes it hard, because I really like seeing his daughter."

She laughed then, and the smile that lit up her face made Aaron feel happy.

"Who knows? He might be let off. He might be able to say that he had no idea what was going on. Regardless, my relationship with him and Mother has been damaged. They won't let me forget that, and I'm okay with that."

"What do you think they'll do?" Aaron asked.

Rosalee frowned in thought. "I think...stay East. After all, they have a good number of friends there. Rumors might get around, but who would believe them? No one there, and no one here."

"I'm sure you are right," he agreed.

"For myself," Rosalee said, and Aaron curled his fingers around hers as she took his arm, "I think I will go wherever my husband goes, and be quite content." She glanced sideways at him. "As long as he's quite sure he can handle a spoiled woman like myself."

"I'm sure he can," Aaron said nonchalantly. "Keeps him on his toes."

"That's good for a man," Rosalee said teasingly.

Aaron stopped walking, and turned to face her. "You're sure you won't regret it?"

"Never," Rosalee said. "My eyes were always drawn to you. I had no idea why at the time. Now I do. It wasn't my eyes seeking you, it was my heart."

"Then say the word," Aaron told her. "We'll marry the moment you are ready."

She nodded, and took his arm again, and they set off down the street. "What about today?"

Epilogue

One year later

"And then, she swung the stick at me and sent me crashing into the side of the wall," Aaron said, staggering about dramatically as he showed what had happened.

Laughter filled the room, and Rosalee marveled, once again, at how genuine it was, and how happy she felt just now. She'd been nervous at first, when her old friend Andrew and his wife Evie invited them to a dinner party, but she really was enjoying herself.

Andrew, her long-time friend, came over to her. "I'm happy you found someone," he told her. "I told you that you deserved to be happy."

"I'm glad we both have that," Rosalee said, smiling first at him, and then at Andrew's wife, Evie, who was taking her turn at telling a story of one of the early moments of meeting Andrew.

"Thank goodness you and I didn't mess things up too badly," Andrew said quietly. "It was quite touch and go there for a few moments with Evie."

"The same," Rosalee sighed. "But, Andrew, he was willing to sacrifice his life for mine. I never imagined such a thing. I'd already fallen in love with him, but that..." She shook her head. "I'm glad you turned me down."

"I am too." Aaron grinned, coming up and slipping his arm around her.

"Yes, though I am sorry for all of the stress you've gone through," Evie said, her warm eyes looking sympathetically at Rosalee. "I know what it's like to have family betray you. It's like no other kind of pain."

"Luckily," Aaron said, "we get to choose our friends, and having good ones like you makes all the difference."

"Here, here!" Andrew agreed, and held up his cup.

Rosalee smiled, letting her eyes drift around the room at the crowd. She hadn't been among so many people since just before her father had sent her away to be married. With the spectacles she wore, she was able to see everyone there quite clearly too. If only she'd been able to see so well in the past, and known what kind of a man her father was.

Currently, as far as she knew, her parents were back East, still running their businesses, living their lives much the same as they always had. She'd sent a few letters, but none had garnered a reply. It was her assumption that her parents had cut her from their lives.

That was quite fine with her. Though it was painful at times, and Evie was right, it was a special kind of betrayal when it was done by a family member, each day the hurt was a little less.

She and Aaron were doing quite well. With his hard work, and only a small part of her inheritance, they'd found their own place, about a half hour from Andrew and Evie, where Aaron was determined to restart his horse breeding business. It was a good location, about equal distance to Cottonwood Falls, Spring Falls, or Hackberry Falls, so he would have many opportunities to sell his horses.

Tonight, several people had approached Aaron, asking for their names to be put on a list for foals. It would only be a matter of time before he was well known for his skill and success in breeding horses, Rosalee was sure.

"Ready to go?" Aaron asked.

"I am," Rosalee told him, and pushed her spectacles a little higher on her nose.

"Those suit you," Andrew told her, as she hugged him goodbye. "So does Aaron."

Rosalee felt a lump in her throat as she smiled at him, squeezing his hand before she turned and kissed Evie on the cheek. "Thank you for inviting us," she said.

"We'll see you soon," Evie said. "Be safe on the way home."

Rosalee waved goodnight, and then she and Aaron went outside and settled into their wagon. The sky was cloudless, and the stars that were scattered above shone brightly. As the horse hooves sounded against the dirt road, Aaron mused, "I never will get tired of this."

"The wide-open skies?" Rosalee asked, tipping her head up.

"No, being with you," he said.

Even after a year, her cheeks pinked at his compliments. "That's lucky for me then," she answered.

"Lucky for me too," he told her. "I'm sure glad you got off at that stage stop and were so stubborn about getting back on."

"So am I." Rosalee leaned into him. She thought about saying more, but everything that could be said had been already, and the things her heart spoke didn't need words.

She never imagined that she'd be here, where she was. Life had given her so many twists and turns, and they'd not always been easy to get through, but she wouldn't change the outcome for anything. Rosalee let her eyes close. There was no need to worry if she did. This was no dream. All she'd ever wanted was right here, with Aaron.

Note from Author

Thank you for taking the time to read *Rosalee*.
Could I ask for one small favor? Reviews like yours on
Amazon mean so much to me and help others to find my
books! Even just a single line means a lot!
Also...
Want a FREE book?
Stop by my website to get your no strings attached **FREE
book**. It's my gift to you, as a thank you for reading this
one.
www.sarahlambbooks.com

Keep reading

If you enjoyed this story, you might also like to read Andrew and Evie's story, and experience the conversation where Andrew reject's Rosalee's offer of a marriage of convenience. Find that in *To Overcome Betrayal.*

At what point does a misunderstanding turn into a lie?

Evie Brown would do anything for her uncle, the only family she's ever known. So when he comes to her with a desperate plea to help save his home and business, she takes the only job she can find—housemaid for a rancher she knows nothing about. Making friends with a ranch hand who literally sweeps her off her feet is just a bonus.

Andrew Radcliffe is tired of every woman he's ever met only interested in his money. Giving up on love, he focuses on expanding his ranch, and demanding loyalty from those who work for him. Mistaken by Evie for a servant in his own home, he plays along. At first, he enjoys the chance to learn more about the spirited young woman working for him. But complications arise as he falls in love with her.

Just after Evie admits to Andrew she's fallen for him, her uncle arrives with a scheme. Now Evie faces an impossible choice—lose the man she's fallen in love with, or turn her back on her family. Who will she betray? And when Evie discovers Andrew isn't just a ranch hand, she's certain no matter her decision, a happy ending is heartbreakingly out of reach.

https://www.amazon.com/Overcome-Betrayal-Hearts-Wounded-Spirits-ebook/dp/B0CYYFK6CK

***

Want to read Dr. Edward Mason's story, of how he and his wife Caroline met?

Caroline Watson has been living at Mrs. Hardy's School for Girls since she was orphaned. When forced into marriage by the headmistress, she plots a desperate escape the night before to the furthest place her money will take her.

Even as he tells himself he is uninterested in the beautiful brunette who appeared off the stagecoach like an angel, Dr. Edward Mason finds himself attracted to Caroline. Still, he's determined that no one is going to tempt him into a relationship ever again.

Pushed together, Edward offers Caroline a job. Just as she's comfortable and settled in, a strange man comes to town and follows her. Now she's faced with a choice. Ask for help or run again.

https://www.amazon.com/Caroline-Runaway-Brides-West-Book-ebook/dp/B0B2N32YP5

About the Author

Sarah writes captivating characters and clean romance that's anything BUT boring! From heartbreaking moments to heartwarming tales, get swept away in either historical or small town romance that pulls you in until the last page.

Nestled in the Blue Ridge Mountains of Virginia where she's married to her Texan husband, you'll find Sarah creating her next book, homeschooling her two boys, or volunteering in her community.

Want more books?

Find them all on Amazon!

https://www.amazon.com/stores/Sarah-Lamb/author/B098H3SGLK

There are other great books in this series as well!

Find all the Boarding House Belle books on Amazon!

https://www.amazon.com/dp/B0F2G2JPXR